A brave new world

Merlin Gideon Gray

A brave new world

Merlin Gideon Gray

2021

ISBN: 979-10-97524-13-5

Novel published by Foxdown Editing under code #2A1304.

Cover art by Emry F. Vresics (@Madam_Mushrooms on Instagram)

More details available at:
Merlingideon.com

Other books edited by The New GRAY Clan:

Chroniques d'une âme en peine
Fur, Fang Claw : Becoming series.
Becoming
A Fox of Hope

Les Etoiles

Aether Walkers

My thanks go to those who walk the path of life with
a smile,

Those who see the sky not as a limit but as a long-
lost lover,

Those who weave with the strings of dreams born
out of their imagination.

To you I send my regards for you make this world
beautiful.

A New Language

As they thought things would happen, well, so they did. Not exactly as I was hoping, but they did in any way. Oh, that's true, you have no idea what I'm talking about... Well, how should I really start this?

Things started changing in my life only a few days ago, as in before that I was living a life anyone could. Not something special, not something out of legends, no magic, nothing. Just a boring old mundane life like any other one you've heard of. And here I am today, in front of the bulletin board at my university seeing that I've been accepted into the translation Master's degree I wanted to enter. It's very new, we are the first year to take it, and very well prepared. Some very well-known translators are going to mentor us, the only downside: you need three languages. That is not a problem in itself, it just means that I have to learn another language in the next three months. That's clearly going to be much harder than I would have anticipated, especially considering the fact that I'm going to be learning Norwegian and it's not an easy language. Now, why on earth am I telling you all this you may wonder, basically because that is what is forcing my entire existence to change.

The how now, well it's pretty basic, I need to learn a language so I went to find a mentor, a teacher actually but I called him Master in the first sentence I said so that is him new name. Yes, I am an idiot sometimes. Only sometimes I promise.

So, I went to the Nordic languages section and asked around for a teacher who could give me a crash course in my new language that I have to learn. Obviously, that is not what they want to do with their spare time and even less so near to the end of the year when they have hundreds of papers to correct. Yet, after much research and annoying the secretaries I get a response, by email. I mean seriously, I sent out at least twenty emails and then went around all the offices, and then they give me a response by email. Sorry, I'm ranting.

The reply is brief as all heck:

'Hello Dear Student.

Come to office ML 135 at 5:35 pm today. I shall mentor you. Do not be late.'

Yeah, alright, well that's sorted. And gives me two and a half hours to brush up all my good reasons for him/her to tutor me. I have no idea who this professor is, I've never seen the surname and there was no first name. All things taken into account, this can probably go really well or really very bad. I just need to hope it's the first one of those two. I don't really have the courage to learn a language on my own and get it right. Now I need to wait and see what is going to happen. In the mean time, maybe I should actually tell you who I am.

My name is Roarn Rogue, I'm a dude, your average type dude, nothing special. Long curly brown hair with gold streaks, eyes green-brown-gold and whotheheckknowswhat. I'm 1m80 and weight I don't care how much, enough that it's still hard to pull myself up the wall when I'm at the climbing hall. If one starts to think too much about all these things, it starts to look like an autobiography and I'm really not here for that, sorry. I'm just giving you a few pointers so that you know what to look for in the street if you want to meet me one day. Okay, nope, that's also a joke, it's just for you to have a general idea of what I look like.

Let us get back to the real reason why I'm writing all of this down; the change in my existence. Not the learning a language part, the bit that happened when I go to see the famous mentor. I've been thinking about it quite a bit and nothing seems very conclusive as I have no idea who this person is. I'm expecting anything from an earful because I was annoying him asking around all day, to a life-changing crash course. The dashingly not amazing thing about this is that, no matter what I expect, it's probably going to be something else. So let me just sip my coffee and we'll talk again in a couple of hours.

Yes, yes and yes again, I know you are reading this so a line does not equal two hours but to me it does so there. Live with it, seriously!

Well, it's now 5:34 pm and I'm in front of the door to the requested office, that looks more to be a broom closet but hey, poor unlucky teacher, I guess. Just as I'm about to knock a voice from inside calls out 'come in you are only 7 seconds early'. It's a woman's voice, and a young one at that.

So, I let myself into the tiny office, close the door and find myself so close to the teacher that I can feel her breath on my face. What the heck is that about!

- 'Hello, I hear you're looking for a super-powerful crash course in Norwegian, is that right?' She asks me, still not stepping back in the slightest.
- 'Yes, that is the case. Will you be teaching me?' I ask in a half-sheepish voice. I'm not really used to have anyone other than my partner this close to my face; not even my best friend.
- 'Oh, well I suppose I will be yes. But not just a language, I'm going to try and teach you a lot more than that. The first of which is manners: brush you damned teeth, your breath smells like the fur of a walrus bum.' I was not expecting that, but then it's true that her breath does not smell of anything, not your typical mint from toothpaste or anything.

- 'Apologies, that is the inconvenient part of being at university all day, I shall remedy to it before our next encounter.' I don't even have time to finish that she is butting in.
- 'Also, you will not apologize, ever, for anything.' She is now looking at me right in the eyes, and now only do I realize her eyes are an impossible purple colour. 'Also, this meeting was only the first, all others will happen in the mornings, early, and at night, late.'
- 'Then we will not have access to the university if I am not much mistaken. Where would you like to meet?' I still have no idea if this is a good idea but have no choice in the matter, I must make it be good, that's all I can do.
- 'We shall meet by the castle and do your lessons in the ancient Greek style; we will walk around, from park to park and then to the university for opening times or, in the case of the night classes, I shall walk you to your home.' She now smiles at me and takes a seat behind what is supposed to be her desk, I suppose. It looks more like a filling cabinet but that does not matter, I guess. She then gestures for me to sit and I sit on what was a stool, at least a few eons ago.
- 'What may I call you?' I have not even given her my name and neither do I have hers.
- 'You shall start by calling me by my rightful rank and first name, one day maybe you will be allowed to use just my name. It all depends on your progress. For now, I

am Master Oska to you.' She then gives me a Cheshire grin and says: 'And what must I call you?'

- The urge is too strong: 'Apprentice of Master Oska or AMO for short, and if the situation requests a bit more etiquette, then you can use my name.' I smile, she does too and then goes on.
- 'And what is your name AMO? The one you were given by your parents that is.' Damned, can't fool around with that.
- 'Roarn Rogue is my name. But AMO is cool too. It's as you wish Master Oska.'
- 'We shall see, for now we need to start your classes!'
- 'Yes Master.'

Those are the last words I can say for almost an entire hour. She does not let me talk. At all. Ever. She is the Master; I am the apprentice and thus I must be silent. The scary thing is what all she tells me in that hour, what we are going to be learning is a ton and a half more than just a language. She is planning on teaching me what the true history of earth is and what sort of things some rare individuals are capable of doing. Apparently, there is magic and some sort of thing she is calling by a strange word. It's almost like 'tkixsi' or something like that; it's apparently a name for energy. I had no idea and I'm not even sure I want to believe it. If it was not for the fact that she is actually going to teach me Norwegian at some stage, I would have left the room by now.

After a long hour of me being forced silent, she asks me directly: 'Will you be a true apprentice and learn everything I teach you?' I don't have the energy to fight off the fact that it's absolutely absurd and impossible to believe so I just nod in the affirmative. She makes me repeat after her: 'I Roarn do accept to be a faithful apprentice in the ways of the Earth Children and shall not speak of my classes to anyone…' I stop her there and ask if I may tell my soul mate and she nods, makes me start the oath again and adds the rest. '… but my soul mate, of anything that I learn. I shall have but one Master and she shall be Oska Leyveine.' On those words, the last ones of the oath, she gives me an enormous book and tells me I have three days to read it.

The book, or rather codex is at least three thousand pages long but, just as I want to object and say it's impossible, she tells me to stop and that all is possible. Right after that, she gives me a leather pouch, empty save for a glass marble. We then head out of the campus, it's long past closing time but the locks do not lock in just out.

We walk in silence out of the campus and all the way to the huge medieval castle next to it. There she sets our next meeting point, by literally making a dot of fluorescent green paint on the floor. 'You shall be here in exactly seventy-two hours having read that entire codex, having made sure your breath is liveable and wearing something warm and comfortable.' She then gives me a very strange hand gesture and says, 'Good Night AMO.'

I reply in kind and then head home; I have a lot of work to do.

Learning a Lingo Part 2

No, I'm not going to write down everything I've been reading for the past 48 hours but, if you want the main gist of the thing read on. Let me just say that it's a codex on the manipulation of energy and also on the learning of languages and, well many more things. The list is long but one thing I can surely tell you is that it contains many things I don't believe will work, not one little bit. I've been learning a lot of theory and thankfully the codex is easier to read than I thought it would be. There are many very useful pointers on how to memorize better at the beginning and I've been applying them since; to the extent of memorizing everything I read. The type of memory it teaches you is so strange I would not trust myself to explain it to you, sorry. Maybe I could tell you it's a combination of all your senses that you back up onto your subconscious, as if it were a vulgar hard drive out of a PC. The logic of the entire thing, according to me, simple AMO, is that I'm going to be learning a lot more than this soon. So much so that I need a memorization method that is fast enough to allow me to follow whatever Master Oska sends my way.

I did not really want to own up to this bit but I have to tell you something; I've been skipping all the useless classes at university to be able to study the codex. Even with the new memorization technique, I still have to spend at least a full five to ten seconds per page. The ones that have complicated diagrams and annotations on them I have to spend, at times, almost as many minutes on. In retrospect, it's not bad at all; there are only about a thousand pages left and I still have about 24 hours before the next meeting with my master.

Another, potentially juicy, bit of information, is that Eliya, my partner, has been learning with me. She is currently living at my apartment with me; it's called the Nest by the way. We've been spending a lot of time going over the bits we don't understand together and also, after Master Oska contacted me, Eliya will be coming to the lessons when she can make it.

- 'Tell me Roarn, did you get this bit with the convection of energy into a portal? It seems like it allows the user to create portals from one place to another.
- It would seem that is the case but I really don't think any of this stuff actually works, so I have no idea if it's really worth memorizing.
- We've been there Roarn, just learn it all, try and understand as much as possible and then we will ask Master.

- Yeah, I know Eliya but it all seems pointless if it does not work. Don't you find?
- We can just learn it all for now and see with her later, come now. Just explain this bit to me it's not in a language I know.
- It's in Norwegian I think, there were quite a few sections in it, wait I will try and decipher it. It says: For this to work you need to see both the point of origin and the destination. Why the heck does it have to be in a lingo I am only just learning, I don't know?
- Maybe she made it specially to teach you the language? I mean that is exactly why you asked to be mentored so it would be logical that it starts to actually teach you the language.
- There is that I guess. You know, if you go through with this, you're going to be learning a new language too. I hope you don't mind.
- You are my soul mate, so I'd better be able to talk whatever language you can communicate in. I will learn it all. That, and the magic the book is trying to teach us.
- Then let us learn!'

From there on we spend hours reading, comparing our understandings and then reading more. There is so much raw data in this thing that I don't even know how it's possible for my brain to understand it all. Though we are managing to learn it all, memorize it all and even understand some of it.

It has now been nearly a full seventy-two hours; we are at the meeting point, finishing the last few pages of the codex while Master Oska arrives. I don't know if we have to give it back to her or how exactly it works but I'm mainly hoping there will not be another five hundred of these. We have now reached the last page and our master pulled an awesome joke on us: 'I'm going to be fifteen minutes, forgive me you two.' Says the last page. Wait, what? How can she know there are two of us? I was alone when she gave me the codex. Well, no matter what, we have fifteen minutes to flash test each other on what we learnt.

Starting with the learning technique and ending with these famous portals, we are apparently capable of throwing around like mages out of a fantasy book. Well, whatever, it's cool to think that there is an infinitely small chance that it's not bull and that we can really do it. I've been repeatedly asking Eliya where she would want to go first and her response was the sweetest thing ever: 'As close to you as I can.' That's just way too adorable, I want it to work now. *Well, then stop wondering and cast a bloody portal you silly AMOs. And yes, telepathy is your next lesson. And yes two, I can read your every thought but I will not as it is illegal where I come from.* 'And sorry I am late dear students. Well met Eliya, sorry for intruding your mind space but I had to at least prove what you are learning actually works. Now if you please, step into the portal to your left. No one else can see it don't worry.' She is not even here; as if the telepathy thing was not scary enough, she does not even need to pitch up here. Also, how can she not be here if one is supposed to see the place of destination of the portal to be able to use it. *Just use the damned thing, I'll answer all that later. It's hard enough as it is to keep it invisible and open. Move it you two.* No discussing that, we both walk through the shimmering black pool to our left. So that's what a portal looks like, a shimmering pool floating in mid-air. It grows as we walk up to it, just enough for us to fit through and then it's as if there is an invisible and very short path from here to wherever. It is so short one pace is enough to cross the distance. While 'in' the portal, it feels as if we are in a fast forward tube of everything from the castle to I don't know where. It's morning here so we travelled really far and it's also far too warm to be in Normandy.

- 'You're going to have at least a thousand questions, I know, but let me talk first. You are currently in a protected location, on an island in the Pacific Ocean not far from the coast of Japan. I cast those portals using a technique I will be teaching you quite soon that works on atmospheric bouncing and a lot of physics. Also, we are all currently speaking a language the codex was teaching you.
- May I speak,' I ask?
- 'You just did so continue, even if I suppose you want to know what the language is and how you can be speaking

it without thinking.' She is grinning at me because that's exactly my questions but let's make it fun.

- 'I would like to know how it's possible to learn an entire language in a single book. And how come we are using it and not another, more native language.'
- 'It's a protected location, protected from anything not perfectly pure. In other words, nothing other than Earth's original language can be spoken here. Also, nothing other than pure natural energy will allow you to get here. And the reason why you could learn it so fast is because you actually instinctively know it you just needed to unlock that part of your mind.' She gestures for us to follow her and then leads us to a huge driftwood table where there are many more books, and a few pairs of strange objects.
- 'May I ask what all of those are and what the marble you gave Roarn is for?' Asks Eliya in a shy little voice.
- 'All in due time AMO number two. All shall be clear soon. Now listen and listen well.'

Those are her last words in anything I could understand. The rest is a series of strange sounds that my body responds to but I don't understand at all. The next thing I know I'm going through a form of pain I don't even know how to explain in words. My entire body feels as if it is burning up. Something is clearly changing and it takes pain for it to happen.

After what feels like ten good minutes, the pain comes to an end and then come a strange feeling of euphoria.

'You are both going through the first level of purification. It's my world making you pure enough to live in it. It will only be painful for this part; the others will happen in your sleep. It will remove all the toxins you have ingested and assimilated in your lifetimes. Also, you will soon learn to do this yourselves. Now, follow me, we have work to do and it's getting late back there.' She makes us take one of each gismo and pack them in our pouches, gives us a pile of books each and then walks off into the jungle.

We continue walking down a well-worn path for at least ten minutes before ending up at the other side of the island in a huge bay. There is a tiny village made up of a dozen or so houses all built on stilts. There are many platforms in the trees so I guess that's where the rest of the village is. Everyone here greets Master Oska with reverence and clearly stare Eliya and I down. They are all speaking in the language of the earth or whatever it's called and are bluntly saying that it's a lost cause to bring new people into the community. We reach a house in the centre of the little village and are ushered in.

'Greetings Lord Trevner, these two are my apprentices and need to be prepared to receive their marks please.' Says Master to the old man in the hut house.

He does not reply but does nod and gestures for us to sit down. Master Oska smiles at us with what seems to be pride and then I black out.

Community service?

Next thing I know, when I'm back in the world of the alive, there are a few very strange prickly feelings going up and down my arms. Not in a way you would think, nothing bothering or unpleasant, just a very present hum of something under my skin.

- 'Roarn are you awake? You two have been out for a few hours already, you need to get back to your place or decide to sleep here.' Master Oska is leaning over us and beaming down as if we were her prodigy children.
- 'I don't know, what do you think? When will Eliya wake up?' My voice sounds strange, it's full of sounds that were never there before. I have no idea what on earth they did to us.
- 'She will be awake soon. And I would recommend you go back now to avoid being dead tired tomorrow in class. Also, you don't want to strain your bodies so, with your authorization, I will open the portal directly into your apartment.
- Go for it, but don't you need line of sight for the portals to work?

- I do, but you can send one portal through another and thus create a tunnel from the start point to the destination.
- Oh, well that is cool. Does it take a long time to be able to do that sort of thing?
- All depends on your mastery but it should be one of the first things you learn. The young ones here learn it in their first-year classes.
- You guys are noisy! Let me sleep.' That would be Eliya waking up.
- 'Hello Eliya, as you're awake I shall portal you two back to the Nest as you call it. Also, our next meetings will be set during the week.' Master Oska then goes out of the hut we are in and only then do I realize we are wearing very little.
- 'Maybe we should get dressed before leaving, don't you think.' I ask my soul mate.
- 'What happened to us? I feel as if I've got an entire world of electricity under my skin.
- I have no idea; it feels like that to me too but it also feels right.
- Yeah, I know right. Maybe we should ask Master before we leave.'

We get dressed, not with our clothing but with some very fine and very nice linen cloths. Once we are both ready, we go outside and there we find Master Oska making a backpack ready with all our books and other things. She ushers us over and gives it to us. 'Everything you need is in here. We'll see each other tomorrow at university. Sleep well you two.' And on those words, she throws, yes literally, a portal over us. Next thing I know we are in my apartment.

We slept almost immediately once we got home, class starts at ten this morning but Eliya's internship starts at nine so the poor girl has to go there really early. While she gets ready, we practise voluntarily speaking in the language of the Earth Children. Master did not tell us the language's name or anything useful about it. We manage to get a full conversation in that lingo before Eliya has to leave. I then start reading the next codex from our pile before going to translation class. There are many interesting things in this one; most of which revolve around the manipulation of our energy and what is doable with it. Apparently portal magic and the other magic are in fact one and the same; all of it works by applying energy to things, places and moments. I've not even read a hundred pages yet that there are already huge sections in Earth Child language and others in Norwegian. I suppose that was to be expected considering the fact that I originally approached Master Oska so that she would teach me that language, not to be embarked on an inter species adventure of a lifetime.

After half a day of class, I go down to the bookshop where Eliya is interning and we have lunch together while practicing, as best as we can, our linguistic talents and talking about what we expect our next lessons will be about. She goes back to work and I go back to class for the last hour or the day. Then, I will spend all the time till my sport session working on the codex and trying to understand the use of the different gadgets we were given.

Good day Roarn, would you come to my office please, I know Eliya is working you can fill her in later? Make it fast, I'm teaching in seven minutes.

I hurry over to Master's office and let myself in. I am not even surprised when I find her, sitting on her desk, crackling with black energy like her portal.

- 'Listen, I don't have much time. You need to be available this evening from 7 till at least 10. I'll portal you from the castle like yesterday. Don't bring anything with you and don't be late.' She seems really stressed out and only now is her energy dissipating.
- 'We will be ready Master Oska, should we wear the clothing we were given yesterday?
- Yes, that would be a good idea; also, if you have time to find one, bring a dagger or a knife or something sharp, you'll need it.
- All right. Why was your energy crackling like that and why is it black?

- It was crackling because I just used a lot of it and it is black because that is its colour. It's something to do with the fact that I'm a nocturnal person or something.
- Oh, that's complicated. What colour is mine?
- You'll see soon enough don't worry. Now, I need to go teach. See you later AMO.'

She pushes me out her office, shrugs off the coat she was wearing and dashes off into the distance. Before I forget I send Eliya a message telling her about all this, she finishes at 7 p.m. usually so it's going to be hard for her not to be late.

Making it, only just on time, to the meeting point, the portal appears and we jump through. You are probably thinking by now that we are really crazy to point blank trust all of this and just play along not asking any more questions. Well, think of it this way; there has been no reason to think it was a bad idea so it's easier to make it a good idea. It's just that there has been so much proof that everything Master is teaching us is true that it's silly to refute it. I'll leave that aside for now, you can decide if you want to think we are crazy or if it's okay to just follow the adventure train.

We are in a different place to last time, we left in daylight and are now in the middle of the night. Also, the air does not smell as clear and clean as the previous place. I think this is just a normal human place nothing special about it. Master is there waiting for us with a little bag each and two sheets of paper each. She does not say a word more before disappearing into the portal we came from. We immediately read the pages and surprise; they are in Norwegian. We run over them as fast as we can and basically, it's a list of things to do. It's like reading a cookbook but for something a lot stronger than your average cake. This, as far as I understand is union magic, protection magic and purification magic. It's not exactly the most explicit sort of thing and more than being cryptic or not, it's plain common hard to read it all. There are charts absolutely everywhere on the page and I don't understand half of them. Yet, between the two of us, we manage to read the instructions, the rules for the casting of the various magic and then we get to work. The funny bit is that it clearly says we are doing community service by accomplishing this work. I wonder what that means to them. Cleaning up a beach is definitely good for the community but what sort of community is it?

We start casting the five spells, in the right order, with everything set up like it should be and then we join it all together with the union spell. It's funny that one of the things this spell needs is a kiss; it says 'kiss your soul mate'. We obviously follow the instructions and next thing we know there is no more murkiness in the air, no more dirty water on the beach, everything is clean, pure and sweet. It goes a lot faster than I would have hoped too; I thought it takes ages for these spells to work.

It does, you two just went overkill on the energy you put into the spells. Good job, though, the report just came in, apparently you went as far as clearing the entire little island. I'm sure the locals will be happy with your work.

Well, I hope so because it sure took a kick out of me, good thing I did not work too hard on anything recently. I've actually got a load of energy to spare so that helps somewhat. Now, as for the rest of the daily events, we need to get back home.

Not just yet, I think you need to rest a bit first. Your energy levels must be extremely low at the moment. Take some time to read and rest, I'll portal you back to your nest a little later. You can sleep safe and sound where you are, it's a secure location. Maybe, it's a bit early, but you guys should get your marks. As if I'm supposed to know what that means. We were apparently prepared for them but were never told what they are going to be. I'll just start reading the rest of the books we have.

- 'Roarn, do you think we should take turns to sleep while the other reads. We can set ourselves into that strange learning sleep mode. If this magic works, which I still can't believe by the way, then that should work too, I guess.
- Yeah, you sleep first I'll read out loud for you to learn. I must say it is pretty amazing that we just cast magic

spells, I'm not used to feeling my fantasy world join the real one.

- I'm still scared I'm going to wake up and this is all going to be one seriously amazing dream.
- Same here. You sleep my dearest, I'll start with the codex on transmission.
- Alright, don't forget you can read really fast it's not a problem.
- Sure thing. Sleep tight, love you.
- Love you too.'

And just like that she falls asleep. I start reading out the codex, fast, very, very fast. I must be reading at somewhere around 300 words per minute. I did not even know my mouth could do that. I'm having to drink every ten pages but at least it's going fast and we are both remembering it all. When, on the hundredth page, I realize this codex teaches you how to do telepathy, I start to want to experiment with it and do exactly that. The only thing is, rather than hearing Eliya's thoughts, I hear some animal's thoughts. At least I think it's an animal because it's all very hyper, very fast and full of feelings not words. In a way, the animal is also speaking the language of the Earth Children, it's just so fast I can't understand what it is saying. I try to mentally slow it down but then it is just too much information and I lose concentration. Not wanting to wake Eliya too early, I continue reading, still very fast, and

make it almost halfway through the codex before she
awakens.

- 'That learning and sleeping thing really works. It feels as
  if you printed the codex right into my mind. It's
  amazing!
- Yeah, and did you try the telepathy thing? I could only
  hear animals; I could not hear your thoughts at all.
- No, I did not yet, let me try.'
- Does this work? I can hear your thoughts. It's really
  funny, I even know that you really want to poop.
- 'Yep, it works and yep, I do, and no I can't answer you
  or at least I don't think so.' I have to answer out loud
  because I can't talk back to her.
- Why not think to me? I could hear those words before
  you said them, so try.
- Well, do you hear this? I am jealous, I only got to hear
  the thoughts of some hyper animal.
- Yep, I hear you just fine, loud and clear. And don't be
  jealous, it will come in time, I'm sure. It all works out in
  time.
- If you say so. For now, it's my turn to sleep.
- 'I'll telepathically read the next bit to you, maybe it will
  go even faster.' She says.

I fall asleep with my head on her legs and the next
thing I know I'm in a vivid dream full of formulae and text.
It's all perfectly clear and perfectly understandable so I guess

this is what it feels like to be uploaded to. It's pretty amazing and feels almost like a strange mental tickling. I manage to get all of it memorized while I know that my body and conscious mind are resting. The only thing I need to do is read and repeat everything as it comes into my mind.

The formulae take me much further than simple telepathy; they explain how to unlock and lock various parts of the mind and also how to force one's brain into cooperation with another. It's a form of linking magic that is so powerful it needs twelve days to fully cast. Eliya wakes me up not long after that bit and I'm back into the real world.

With both of us rested, Master Oska sends us a portal for home and we hop through.

Stranger Stuff

Five more days went by with a lot of sleeping and reading, there is so much to learn and so little time apparently. Master keeps on telling us that we are far too slow and that the world needs us. Also, apparently there are going to be more students joining us soon. I still can't seem to telepathically talk to any human and I figured out that the animal from last time was a very excited squirrel. That's really all I needed isn't it, to be wired so strangely I only hear animal thoughts? At least the codex taught how to block out thoughts and how to protect our minds before they taught us to open up and communicate. It helps that I'm not constantly hearing the thoughts of every animal in the vicinity, that would have driven me crazy within moments and you don't want me crazy, trust me, I'm annoying enough as it is. *No, you're not, now come we have work to do.* And yes, so we do.

We are currently working on a very old codex that is all about the true history of earth. Maybe this I should actually tell you…

Let's start the basic way, the beginning:

Earth was created about 12,000 years ago along with the rest of the universe, yes hard to believe if you still think evolution & it's buddy the Big Bang are true. I'll let you read the book of Genesis if you want more details on how it happened but I'll give you a few bits you'll have a hard time finding. Firstly, Adam and Eve spoke the language the Earth Children speak; it is the language of creation itself. The words are the real names and descriptions of the things in the world. What the Earth Children are, well I guess I should call them the children of Abel. When his brother Cain killed him, Abel did not die with his ideology of peacefulness, which lives on to this day. The people who followed this ideal, stayed as close as possible to the ways of their ancestors and as close as possible to Eden itself. What this resulted in was a scission of the people, the followers of Cain and the children of Abel. The followers of Cain became the humans we all know and the children of Abel are the Earth Children. There are very few of them and they have been rising and falling in numbers over the years. There has never been more than one per million humans. Now, why do they have magic you're wondering; basically, because they were granted that as a means of protecting themselves. They are the most faithful and close to God people you can imagine, every codex has hundreds of references to him in it. Now, let me not go all religious on you right, back to the history bits.

There are many divisions and groups in the human population and there are also divisions in the Earth Children. Just because they followed Abel's peacefulness does not mean that they are all peaceful at heart. Once you have spells strong enough to wipe out cities, it becomes hard not to be tempted to do so. The devil is also mentioned here but I'll skip that bit and tell you that some things like plagues and freak storms, earthquakes and landslides, were used by the less savoury Earth Children to rid the planet of humans. It was always stopped and thankfully they never managed but there is always a risk that one day they will be able to launch a global annihilation spell that will not be countered in time. I mean the plagues were violent enough as it is so just imagine if they can make that worse.

Why would they hurt and kill humans you may wonder; basically because, and they are right so hark, humans are killing earth so to protect earth they need to get rid of humans. Okay, I'm not fine with the bit about killing humans but it's true that we are killing earth. I do like the other policy we find in their history: creating beauty in desolate places to show humans that it's possible to live without destroying. I'm sure you've heard of the place where nature shaped itself around human's abandon. The place in Belgium called 'Where cars go to die', that was taken back by nature but with a lot of help from the children. Now, out of the history, Eliya and I are going to be the next generation of children. It's not a genetic thing, it's all a choice and an active one. There is only one counterpart to it all, if we learn how to use magic, we can no longer use technology or live in the human air without needing daily purification.

That's a sacrifice I'm ready to make and so is Eliya; we will live up to what Master Oska expects of us and we shall train the next Children in our stead. It's a lot of work, a lot of sacrifices, and very little real sleep but it's totally worth it.

To add to the strangeness of the all the historical shifts we are having to accept as pure truth, we are going to get our marks soon. Apparently, it is like a gauge marked into one's skin by magic. It allows us to know how much energy we have and where we are in the balance of things; meaning good or bad. The marks are usually given a lot younger but we are late bloomers or something. We have to choose what we want ours to look like and for the moment I'm going for a series or vines and animal footprints wrapped around my arms. I will be getting at least five on each arm apparently. For what I could read about the marks, they have a dual colour balance, we choose only one of the two, the other is a natural opposite of the colour we choose.

While we are working on the various codex Master gave us, Eliya stumbles upon a very interesting snippet of information we had not yet read about. It's nothing as strange as I would have hoped, like the fact that we have an organ no normal people have or something like that. It's just a chapter on elemental linking. What that means is quite simple, each Child is affiliated to an element that, while not necessarily, will be their strongest magic for life. That is different for us, we are still purifying ourselves into being like the Earth Children thus we will only know what our elements are when we start casting pure energy magic like portals.

It's Nothing If Not a Miracle

A few weeks have gone by and so have a few more codices and many more cleaning missions. We have not yet been given our marks but apparently, we'll be ready for them quite soon. As much as I'm looking forward to having them, I'm not sure my parents are going to be too happy when I come home with my arms tattooed. As for my inability to speak to humans with telepathy, it is still as present as ever; the only counterpart for that is that I'm now really able to listen to animal thoughts and not only listen I can talk back. Strangely enough they seem to understand some of the langue of Abel and otherwise sending them pictures or desires works too. I've been repeatedly communicating with a vixen that lives in the forest next to my parent's place. She is a very active little fox and clearly likes being able to talk to someone who is not a male fox trying to make her pregnant all the time. By talking to her in the original language, she is learning quite a lot of it and is managing to make sentences and, well basically to talk. I've invited her to meet me many times, as in for us to see each other upfront but she says it would be a bad idea for some obscure reason.

Eliya has been practicing talking to me from as far as she can manage. With the help of Master Oska, she has been portal travelling across the planet and talking to me when she could. She is currently some place in South America learning to use nature to augment her mental power. The idea is that, when there is lightning, she can use it to channel her thoughts into the atmosphere and then to me. It's not yet been working too well, I only heard one word and it was not reassuring; it was 'shit'. Yeah, I know that could be fine but I really don't think so.

Roarn, get to the hospital right this moment, I don't care how but get here. Eliya got struck by lightning and is in massive pain. We need her soul mate here to help cast the healing spells and to absorb the pain. WELL, SHIT!

I run as fast as I can and try to cast a few acceleration spells and only one works but it's enough to make me run very fast.

Getting to the hospital a quarter of an hour later, I ask for the room where Eliya is and am directed to the heavy care wing of the hospital. That's really not what I wanted, why does it have to be so bad. Dashing, as fast as is possible and allowed in a busy hospital, I find the place I was pointed to and here I am given a room number. Walking up to the door of room 236 the shift in the air is palpable; there are far more spells around here than I would have thought possible in a human hospital.

- 'Roarn, you managed to get here fast well done. We are working with the human doctors, undercover as foreign specialists in electrocution. You don't need to worry she is going to be fine.
- What happened? How on earth did this happen to her? And why is she covered in bandages?
- She is burnt along her legs, back, sides and arms. How it happened, well no one really knows. It's almost as if she called the lightning down herself. There was no natural ark to it; it was like a wire straight into her.
- What damage did it do other than the burns?
- Nothing, in fact, to the contrary, it seems to have altered her magic and made it much stronger than it was. She absorbed a part of the energy. It's a miracle she's not dead and it's technically impossible that she would be able to do what she did.
- Are you telling me that she absorbed lightning itself?
- Exactly Roarn, exactly. She may have more magical power than even the elders. We'll only know later this evening when we wake her up.
- What do the human doctors say?
- Not much, apparently, it's just some hard burns, they did not see the fact that she has been crackling with

energy for hours. Also, I doubt that she will be too happy
to see her hair.

- What's wrong with her hair?
- Take a look.' Master Oska, grimly at first and then more
  sincerely smiles at me and remove a part of the bandage
  on Eliya's head.

Eliya's hair has gone from its lovely golden brown to
nearly transparent snow white. She is going to find that really
strange and I think she'll find the Lichtenberg fractals burnt
into her skin are a little more bothering. I'm starting to
wonder what it will look like once she is entirely healed.
Roarn, can you hear me? Comes her mind voice into my head.
It's so loud I almost cry. I try and think back to her that I can
hear but she does not seem to hear me.

- 'What happened?' Asks a now awake Eliya. She is
  speaking the language of the Earth Children with utmost
  purity. And moreover, her voice sounds different, not by
  much but still.
- 'You were hit by the lightning and it nearly killed you.
  You're in the hospital back at home and your parents are
  on their way. Also, you are in a human hospital so speak
  one of their languages rather.' Answers Master.
- 'Thank you, Master. Can you tell me why my limbs feel
  so strange? It's as if someone is constantly tickling me.
- We think you may have absorbed some of the electricity
  you were shocked by. We'll only know when you go for

your marks or if you cast a spell but for now you need rest and to let your body heal. We'll make sure the burns you are currently sporting heal as much as possible.

- Thanks. I'll just rest; wake me up when my parents get here, please. And Roarn, stop worrying it's hard to block out.' And just like that she drops off to sleep again.

It's funny how she complains about me worrying being hard to block out, considering my brain is still feeling numb from her previous mental jolt. There is nothing wrong with her telepathy, to the contrary, it's so damned powerful that everyone in the hospital probably heard each word she said. Now, the only thing is that we can't really tell her parents what happened and I have no idea what sort of lie will work to get her out of this one. I almost think it will be better if we don't lie but that seems to not be an option seeing the worried thoughts frown across Master's face. I don't want to radiate worry but it's hard to think all is fine when it's possible for this entire situation to go rapidly south. I don't want to think that there is a risk for Eliya's health but that remains a distinct possibility.

- 'Master, what are we going to tell her parents when they get here? You can't expect them to believe us if we say she jumped onto a live high voltage wire.
- No Roarn, we will tell them that she was hit by lightning and that the fact she is still alive is a miracle.

- But there have been no storms here for weeks, how could she have been hit? And please don't tell me we are going to say she was travelling because they would never believe that.
- No, AMO, we will tell them that there was a freak storm and that she was stuck because it happened out in the fields when she was out walking.
- I don't think that will work but I guess there is no way around it.
- It's not a lie, we can't lie. She was out walking, there was a freak storm, and she was struck by lightning. None of that is a lie; it just did not happen here that's all. Unless if they know how to read weather patterns, nothing will give that away so don't worry. And we can talk later, they are here.'

Eliya's parents burst into the hospital room, not really respecting the laws of silence and discretion around the ill but one thing is for sure they are far more worried than I was expecting. I know the whole parents and child thing, especially when the child is the youngest one and all that, but seriously, they are dripping worry. *Hello mum and dad. Sorry my throat hurts a little so I'm going to talk to you like this. Roarn and Master Oska can hear this too. Also, you can talk out loud it's fine.* That will be Eliya making all our scheming about keeping this story secret a bust. Well, now, let's see the reaction. Her parents are staring at each other, then at her, then at Master and me.

- 'What happened? We'll talk about the rest in a minute.' Asks her mum.
- I was out training and I got hit by lightning. I'll let Master explain the training. Replies Eliya.
- 'Since she showed you, she can talk telepathically there is no need to hide the fact that I am training her in magic and the original ways of earth. She is learning all this with Roarn who is also my apprentice.' Replies Master Oska in Earth Child language.
- 'What were you speaking, I understood what you said but my brain tells me you are not talking a language I know? And since when is magic real?' Asks Eliya's mum; she does not seem bothered by the fact that her entire world is changing. Maybe that is due to the fact that her daughter is lying on a hospital bed covered in Lichtenberg fractals burnt into her skin for life.
- 'It's the language of my people, the E'rtkin or Earth Children. We are the descendants of Abel the pacifist son. The language itself has no name as it would be too dangerous to name the language of magic though to make your life easy you can call is E'rtkinian.' Ah ha, so that is their real name and now at least I have a name for the language, even if it's nothing official.

- 'Are you telling me that the bible's mythology is real, that's somewhat hard to believe?' Asks Eliya's dad.
- 'All the legends are true and most of the stories are real. All that is written in the bible is true even if some of it has been a little badly translated. And as for magic, it is our equivalent to your technology.' You should see his face, maybe someone should have told the world all this a long time ago but no one wants to believe that they are wrong so no one would follow this sort of thing.
- Just so that you guys know, I'm going to be healed very soon. I've been chatting with some of the E'rtkin healers and they gave me the spells I need to heal myself. I vote we take this conversation to a nice coffee shop it stinks of disinfectant in here and that's driving me crazy. Eliya's energy starts to crackle slightly as she casts her spells, her voice still sounding far more entrancing than it used to. Her energy is pure white and silver, it's beautiful.
- 'Well, I must say that if you can heal yourself then there is not much to worry about is there. As if. You are going to be staying right where you are until the normal doctors say you are well enough to leave.' Her mum seems somewhat less happy about the situation, to say the least.
- 'Well, I'm fine mum. You can see for yourself.'

With those words Eliya sits up and takes off her bandages before anyone can stop her. Under them is fresh skin and the burnt fractals are now only thin white scars. The one thing that is a noticeable change is the drastic drop in her energy. I can feel that, which means it must be quite the difference. She sits on the edge of the bed and dangles her feet off the side smiling at us. Only then do I think that maybe I should get her some clothing and cover her up. I give her the bits of clothing I was smart enough to bring from the Nest and then we all leave the room for her to change. When the doctors get there and find her pacing around her room ready to go, they almost faint. She was in intensive care for less than three hours and already she is cleared to go out.

The doctors spend almost twenty minutes deciding that she is really fine and let her go while still clearly thinking she is impossible. She should have been in for at least another week. When all the paperwork is sorted out, all covered by Master, we head out and go to the nearest coffee shop.

I'm holding Eliya's hand while we walk and she is constantly giving me very small shocks. It's almost as if, even after having depleted her energy, she still has the electricity in her.

A Magical Tattoo

After a few hours of explanations and a lot of gobsmacked expressions from her parents, Eliya and I finally managed to get ourselves out of there and home. Master Oska telling us that we needed to be ready because our next assignments are going to be due soon. The worst is that there are also my university exams that will happen shortly. So, on top of being busy all the time for my apprenticeship in magic, I also have to finish my bachelor's. I've been thinking of using the speed learning on my classes but it would look too much like cheating if I start getting perfect scores on every test. I'll just do with what I know and hope for the best, my results are usually good so it should work out just fine.

Two days after all those crazy events, after the fifth thousandth hundred million, you get the point, lots, of Eliya's parents calling to know she is fine, we get our assignment from Master Oska. This time it's going to be on a Saturday and we are going to be off the grid for the entire day. Thankfully, Eliya is not working at her internship this Saturday so we can go without worry and do whatever is needed. She has been able to rest quite well these past days and has recuperated most of her depleted energy. I wish we

could learn to transfer energy, that would be really useful and
I want to learn healing spells too.

- 'Roarn, are you done with the codex on personal
  transformations yet? I really want to try that hair colour-
  changing spell.
- Don't you find your silver hair really cool? I like it.
- That's not the point; I would like to have it back to its
  original brown. The silver makes me look strange; I find.
- Oh, all right. And I must say I did like the dark brown
  and gold hair you had so it would be nice if you can get
  it back to the same tint. I'll be done with the codex soon.
  Which one are you on?
- I'm learning the stuff on potions, it's pretty fun. Did you
  know there was a potion that could make you talk
  almost any language for a week? That's really cool.
- I guess they invented that to prevent the E'rtkin from
  speaking their language to outsiders. Well, I would not
  mind you transferring that knowledge to me later on. I'll
  read you the one I'm working on.
- That would be perfect let's do that, but first, what does
  Master want us to have ready for tomorrow?
- She said that we need to prepare comfortable underwear
  and that's it. I don't get the point but hey her commands
  are law, I guess.

- Yeah, okay she is still strange. When do you think we get our marks and what are you going to tell your parents when they see your arms covered in tattoos?
- I'm just going to tell them the truth, your parents know mine should too.
- Good idea, because hiding your marks would be a pain.
- Definitely, it would mean wearing long sleeves at all times and I really don't feel up to that in weather like the current.
- Oh, and when are you meeting your famous vixen? You two are still talking, right?
- We don't know yet, sometime soon I guess and yes, of course, we are still talking. Want me to say hello from you?
- You can do that yeah.'

The famous vixen is the current name for the lady fox I've been talking to every day since I learnt I could talk to animals by telepathy. My range has increased enough that I can now talk to her from fifty or sixty kilometres away which is really nice. As for her, well she is learning so fast that she can now talk E'rtkinian as well as anyone. It's impressive frankly, she is supposed to be a normal fox and yet she can talk to me in a language I understand. That is a clear evolution compared to our first mental exchange that was just bursts of images and feelings. I'm really looking forward to meeting her, it would be fun to actually see the creature I've been talking to for so long in the fur.

Friday came and went so fast that Saturday is already upon us. We are waiting at the usual spot near the castle for Master Oska to send us a portal. As soon as it appears we jump through, wearing, under the rest of our clothing, the most comfortable underwear we have. Not that I would ever think of wearing something uncomfortable, it's still nice not to be bothered by one's clothing.

On the other side of the portal, a lovely prairie is waiting for us and right in front of us is a large stone slab with a piece of parchment on it.

'Instructions for the ceremony of marks:

In the correct order, you are to cast the following spells on yourself and on your partner to reinforce his/hers. If you are alone, a Master will accompany you. Also, for your information, the area you are in is protected by over four hundred spells to keep any magic in and also to grant you the needed privacy. Beware the magic markings are on you for life so be careful when you cast the spells. The final marking, the visible part, will be done by your Master. Last notice before you start, the spells hereafter listed are not explained, you are to have learnt each one of them by now, including the conditions of casting. Happy marking.'

That's going to be fun, the list of spells to cast is on the rest of the page and on the back. They are not numbered or anything so we are going to have to be careful with what we do.

Doing the first ten of so spells is quite quick work, especially considering they don't need anything specific to cast them. No, what starts to be tricky is when the next spells ask for us to join our thoughts. Eliya just lets herself into my mind as if it were a totally open place; I've spent weeks on protecting the thing and she just slips in. I don't mind it coming from her but it's still not reassuring. We cast spell 11 twice each and then go on to spell twelve. This one needs us to picture our energy, another quite easy prerequisite yet we are still a little fidgety and uncertain. We go through the rest of the spells on the front and then flip the page. Now start the complicated spells.

The first spell we are told to do on this side is one of transformation. We need to transform the stone slab into a sculpture together, using union type magic. That's not really a hard type of magic, considering we are natural soul mates. Yes, I forgot to say, Master Oska told us that there was a way to know how compatible our magic was and when we accepted the test, she nearly fell off her chair at the result. We are more than a hundred percent compatible, meaning we are so compatible that our magics fortify each other.

Once we have a sculpture of a baby dragon in front of us, we smile and look at the next spell in the list. All of a sudden, our smile is a lot harder to maintain, the next spell is not even a spell, it's a command: 'Animate your previously made sculpture with no more than two spells.' Not only is animation magic very long to cast it also needs lots of energy, more than the two of us have that's for sure. I guess that's why they say two spells, the first is supposed to be energy magic and the second animation magic.

'Pass me your phone please.' Says Eliya out of the blue. I give it to her and, as she holds it, I see my battery drain almost instantly. She then takes hers out and drains it too. 'I've got enough energy for the animation spell. This way we can keep reserves for the rest of them; there are lots.' And just like that she casts the animation spell, well not instantly, there are nearly four full minutes of chanting the incantation for it to be proper enough. I use the other spell we are allowed to cast a mid-grade regeneration spell on Eliya so that she can get her energy back faster.

We go through the rest of the spells, in order, like they must and, when at last we reach the final one, I understand the reason for the plane and the protection. The last spell is not a spell, it's a quest: 'Cast as many different spells as you can in fifty minutes. A timer will appear as soon as you cast the first one. You may rest for a while before starting. All spell will be worth various numbers of points and your points are in common so work together.'

We rest for a good hour before starting to list as many spells as possible to cast. While sharing our energy over a mental link Eliya opened, we start casting. Speaking as fast as possible, we go through hundreds of spells, thousands even, every single one we know, from the base magic to the hardest ones. We are only halfway to the hard one when we see the point counter hit 100. It did not say anything about how many points we need for us to validate the test. Also, we only have a few minutes left. *Cast a high-level spell. I'll do the same.* And at that we do. I go for a transformation spell and turn our, now animated, stone baby dragon, into a bronze animated baby dragon. It's always fun to know that all I need is a load of energy and I can permute any material into another. I would have loved to try making coal into gold but apparently that sort of magic would kill anyone normal. Eliya is casting a concentration spell, thus making a ball of pure light. I see that our points jumped by a couple hundred so clearly that worked quite well. What worked less well is the fact that we now have a bronze baby dragon flying around the protection dome as if it was its home. I wonder how many of the protection spells around us we have destroyed. Probably quite a few even if they are surely much stronger than anything we can cast.

- 'Well done you two, you beat our expectations. 347 points on the last question is really good work.' Says Master Oska as she appears in front of us. She then signals in a slightly strange way and I see the field we were in disappearing and a village appears in its place.
- 'Where are we? And did we pass the test?' Asks Eliya cutting straight to the point.
- 'We are currently in one of the villages of the E'rtkin as close as we could be to your home town. That is one of the necessities for the marking trials to work. And yes, you managed the trials pretty well, now just call your dragon over please.
- It's a bit complicated considering it's an animated piece of metal. What do you want us to call?' I ask wondering if it's even possible to call an artificially animated creature.
- 'Just do it Roarn, just try.' Master smiles at me with a very warming smile and so I do what she told me to. I call out to the dragon with my mind and find resistance there. Much too strong for an artificial intelligence. I force my way through it and immediately I feel the dragon. I tell it to come to me fast, and it does.
- 'How can it possibly understand commands? It's a fake, there is nothing really alive about this dragon.' I ask after the bronze dragon landed right next to me.
- 'You are right, it did not respond to you, the symbiotic parasite stuck to it did. It's a very dangerous bug we

found millennia ago; it can control anything that can move. And well done by the way.

- But why ask me to call it over? Why bother with the parasite and all that?

- Because you have a gift that is not theoretically possible and so does Eliya so we needed to verify. Animal telepathy is not a normal talent and I'm afraid that it's only the start of your strangeness.' Oh, great so we are not even normal. I never considered myself to be normal but definitely not strange enough for it to be a problem.

- 'What is my gift, Master?' Asks Eliya.

- 'You have the ability to make other energy your own, more specifically electric energy. That's why the lightning did not kill you. Also, electricity is your element. We don't know what Roarn's element is yet.

- What do elements do?' I ask.

- 'You'll see soon, for now you have to go see the marking mage so come.'

That puts a definite end to the conversation for now. We follow Master Oska to a house at the edge of the village under the quite inquisitive stare of the village people. I guess they saw our entire trial, the plain was possibly only a one-way thing. I don't think the marking is going to be fun. I'm even a bit worried it's not just some form of tattoo. *I want the fractal burns on my arms to become my marks*. That would be an interesting format of marking, I'm sure. I'm still going to go for the vines and animal paw prints marks. I did not really think about it that much; a combination of my two favourite things can only be a good choice. *Yes, I think it will be and also, it's going to look cool.*

We arrive at the house and are quietly ushered in by a young girl; she smiles at both of us and then bares her left arm at us. I wonder why until I see the hundreds of tiny geometrical shapes there. Half are blue and half are a beautiful gold colour. I guess those are her marks, they look pretty cool. Did she have to do the same trials as us and if she did how the heck did, she manage all of them at such a young age?

Once we meet the mark's mage, he offers for me to go first as my design is easier to do for him as he has already done both parts. I take off my shirt and sit down on the chair he pulled out, put my arms on the table in front of me and already I feel something strange. The table is made of so many things I wonder how they are all holding on to each other. It's clearly a magical object but what does it do?

He tells me not to move so I try and stay as immobile as possible. Then to my utmost surprise I start to glow and not like a nightlight, like a miniature sun. Then the table starts to glow in five or six sections, and that seems to be abnormal. He looks at Master, Master looks at him and he then starts to chant a spell. Almost as if I was possessed, I feel myself join his spell chanting, repeating his words. They are words of change, of learning, of strength and weakness and a hundred other things I don't quite catch. One thing I pick up is the words 'impossible invocation'. No idea what that means but I do soon feel my arms go numb and then prickly and I want to move but can't. As I look down at my arms, still chanting along with the mage, I see the marks stretch across them exactly like I had pictured them. Spiralling up from my wrist to my elbows, the vines and animal prints, parallel lines repeated four times on each arm. They are black at first and then dark red and dark green. The red is my mark colour for good energy and green for bad energy. There is a basic rule and that is balance; one must have a good balance between positive and negative energy or else it's impossible to cast any form of spell.

Once I have my marks finished, the numbing ebbs away and my arms feel like they have just been burnt to the bone. The pain is so bad I black out almost immediately.

When I come back to the pretty colourful world of consciousness, I am immediately welcomed by a chorus of happy yelps. Wait what? Who the heck is sounding like a fox? *That would be your famous fox. She appeared out of nowhere right before you woke up. She's been sitting on your legs ever since she got here wagging her tail and licking you.* Wait what. I call out with my mind and immediately a very hyper active vixen respond. I open my eyes and see her, the vixen whom I've spoken to so many times grinning at me. Yes, you read that right, she is grinning at me. I mean since when can foxes grin? She clearly can.

- *Hello little fox, how are you doing and how did you get here?* I ask her with my mind.
- *You called out to me and said to come and next thing I knew I was sitting on your sleeping body. And I'm fine thanks, it smells like food out there.* Her capacity at talking to me is much better than ever before and that's when I think I should try learning fox language. But first, how did she get here?
- *Did you jump through something to get here?* It would be a bit more logical if I had used a portal at least.
- *No, you transported me too fast for me to jump onto or into anything.*
- 'Are you two having a conversation or can we ask why the hell a fox is here?' Asks Master.
- 'We are talking yes, and apparently, I transported her here in some strange, not a portal, method. Any insight on what it could be?
- Well, it's not supposed to be the case but I think you have summoning as your element. As in your element is energy itself and your talent is to be able to summon things from one place to another.' What the hell, that is one strange ability? I thought everything was supposed to work on portals, nothing like summoning.

- 'What exactly does that mean? I thought we are supposed to be affiliated to our element and be able to draw energy from it; how am I supposed to draw energy from summoning things?

- It's not a question of affiliation Roarn, you are affiliated to the space you use for the invocation. It's supposed to be a sort of space-time pocket where you can pass a lot of things through. Not everything would work but nearly.

- So, I draw energy when I use energy? Is that it?' That would be the most messed up power I've ever heard of. It would mean that every time I need more energy than I have, it would have to come from another living being. That's just great.

- 'Well, yeah, pretty much, but it means that your invocation magic is your strongest and also least energy costing. Well, we will need to see a specialist in higher magics for us to be sure. For now, it's time for Eliya's marks and I think you might want to take your fox outside.'

Eliya takes a seat at the strange magic table and instead of glowing like with me it dims right down. I tell my fox friend she can go outside and she does. We all look at the marks mage as he starts to cast the spells of his practice. The only thing is, as he does, rather than Eliya chanting with him and making the spell stronger, she is silent and he does not manage to complete even the first part. 'Impossible,' he says.

He looks at Eliya then at me and then at Master Oska before saying we are a strange group. He goes on about it being impossible to absorb magic, even more marking magic. As he rants on and on about how strange and impossible we are, Master sends us out and we thus go and play with my fox friend.

- 'Do you think I'm like some sort of freak and that's why I absorb magic rather than it working on me?' Asks Eliya with a long face. She looks so sad I ask the little Vixen to give her a fox hug and she does. She goes all cat mode on Eliya and licks her like a cub.
- 'I think we are both strange but surely not freaks. Most definitely not in fact. We are just different to what they are used to I'm sure it's nothing bad.
- But I can't even get my marks. That little girl had hers and I can't even get mine. I don't even know why it hurts my ego so much but it really does.
- I understand and don't worry I have no idea what my power is supposed to be, Master hardly explained it.
- Well, here she comes so ask her.'

And so, I ask Master Oska what my power is supposed to mean and she gives me an in-depth explanation of the fact that it is an impossible power and has only been heard of once in the E'rtkin history. It's a sort of crazy mix between the rarest power, energy control, and void magic as well as traces of a few other things like linking/bonding magic and I don't know what else. In other words, take a bunch of crazy magic powers, put them in a cloth bag and squeeze out the juice, I'm what's left. As for Eliya, well it's pretty basic, she has energy magic and void magic linked around her elemental electricity magic. She also has transformation, mutation, alteration, and synthesizing magic. That makes enough different modification things that she can transform any energy into her own. It's apparently not rare to see a mix of elements but never one so strong. Master thinks that she might be strange like this because of the lightning but we will only be sure when we go and see the specialists. That implies going to the capital of the E'rtkin, a hidden city in the middle of Antarctica. It's apparently a beautiful place but a very strange one too. There are years and years of spells piled on top of each other to protect the city, so much so that nothing gets into it, not even sunlight. Only the stars and moon can light it up. Thus, it's a legendary place some human stories tell about but not many.

A Trip to Antartis

Yes, the chapter name is the name of the city, Atlantis was a miss nomination of Antartis the E'rtkin capital. There are very few cities for the Earth Children to live in as they need to fit in between the human places and especially the human pollution. Thus, there are, in total, only four cities, all the rest are tiny little villages or nomad groups even. It's not an easy life to live when you have to purify your air, water, food, everything, just to be able to survive on a daily basis.

We are supposed to go to the capital in a few weeks' time but before then, next week in fact, I have to write a load of exams for university and I have not been studying for them at all. I mean, put yourself in my shoes here, if you learnt that your entire world was only half true and that you could learn about the other half, would you not do that rather than learning about the grammar of the English language. I clearly prefer to learn magic and skills that go with it rather than the phonetics and grammar of English. Not that language learning is boring, it's just that, when you know a language older than any other on earth and that all people instinctively understand; well, it becomes boring to learn something so vernacular. That being said I still need to pass the exams while all my magic classes continue. Apparently, according to Master Oska, we have not even caught up to the E'rtkin our age and will not for a while even by using the immediate memorization techniques and all those fancy things. That does not matter until Eliya has her marks in anyway because, with no way to measure her magic output, it's a bit too dangerous to cast any high-level spells. I don't want her to fall unconscious for days or worse to die from over use of energy. My marks are surprisingly well balanced out; I was expecting a total imbalance in the good and bad energy thing but in the end, they are at a virtually perfect fifty-fifty.

Let me at least give you, my poor reader who has to follow this pace of events, yes, I know I'm in a book, a bunch of details that will not force you to rethink your entire world. First things first, I'm twenty and Eliya is twenty-two, in E'rtkin ages we are both adults but not yet graduates. For that we need to have learnt at least three hundred full codices of base magic, have our marks, past the ceremony of inventive magic and create something spectacular for the royal family. There is not any real hierarchy in their society but they still respect the king and his family as their main law makers and peace keepers. Coming back to being a graduate, well it's going to take us at least a year to study all that we are supposed to but that does not seem impossible.

Now, for other interesting little things. Firstly, I need to tell you that I am no longer going to do the translation

Master's degree but rather one specializing in literature of some sort. Also, my learning Norwegian has become quite slow sadly as I've been busy with the rest of learning. As for my outsideofthestrangeworldofmagic life, let me just tell you that it's full of fun and less fun bits. Eliya and I are planning our wedding that is supposed to happen next year, and that's a very fun source of discussion. Other than that, we have had a lot of things happening, my car's window winder breaking, my student deserting his class as he had better to do with his day, and many more titbits of things. You would think that learning magic is my only concern, well actually I'm currently stressing myself senseless as I lost my one papers, I have to hand-in three days from now. I'm going to die. Nope, I'm going to find another solution and do that. Ha! Thank you brain for working, sometimes that happens, my brain cells usually are at war with each other and don't want to cooperate but sometimes there is a truce.

Talking about a truce, I've recently read that there are quite regularly warlike situations in the E'rtkin world. They are just so careful to the planet that they never let it escalate to a full-fledged fight because that would be dangerous. Think about it this way, some of the oldest mages are able to transform the element they are affiliated to into almost any form they like. If you prefer, that means a simple lighter's flame can be turned into a ball of liquid fire the size of a house. You always need to have your elements on you somewhere if you want to manipulate it. There needs to be some sort of contact. That is why, for someone like me with an undefined element it is virtually impossible to touch it and thus manipulate it. I've not yet tried anything crazy with my summoning yet, I'll go to the forest soon and try it out more in depth.

Moreover, we are still trying the human changing spells to get Eliya's hair back to its previous tint. For the moment that has sadly been quite unsuccessful and she still has stark white and silver hair. They looked at her very strangely when she went to work like that and she said it was a hairdresser doing try-outs. No one questioned it any further, even when she went back the next day with a bit too bright red hair. We are still having to try and change the wording in the spells each time to make the colour right. The problem being that the spell starts with a command translatable as 'Remove change restriction on body'. As in, you can change anything on your body with whatever you say next. That makes for a lot of fun actually, like making each other have multicolour toenails and so on. Of course, one has to be careful and we are extremely wary of danger but it's sometimes that little but too fun to miss out on. Because of my upcoming holidays I'll be spending time at HQ, my parent's place, and thus I'll go to practise my magic in the forest with my fox friend. Eliya has to work and thus stay in the city, it's a pity considering we work better together but it's not so bad considering she can mentally link to me while there.

Master Oska did not give us any information about what the rest of our classes will be about. I hope that Eliya will see the elder of whatever he is, specialist dude for her marks. Being unmarked means that, no matter what she learns, she can only cast spells that have their energy measured and marked in the codex; basic things and a few mid-level spells but definitely nothing in the higher tiers. After studying the magic tiers, I found out that there are in fact a lot more levels than I thought. The highest tier of magic is called 'pure creation', in other words, creation itself. God's power if you prefer. Then there is a huge gap and you reach E'rtkin magic of which the highest is called legendary magic. Followed by, from strongest to least powerful, mythical, parliamentary, Master, top tier, high tier, mid tier, lower mid tier, low tier, base. That makes a lot of different levels but don't worry I'll ask the author to make a memo at the back of the book or something like that.

The human transformation spell is a cross-tier spell as it starts in the top-tier level and can be altered up or down. All depends on what transformation one tries to do afterwards. For instance, changing your eye colour is mid tier; whereas changing your body shape is parliamentary magic. Parliamentary magic being possible to cast only by parliament members or people of the mythical and legendary tiers. There are apparently only very few in E'rtkin history who achieved that sort of level and few are still alive. The current high rank in the magic world is the parliament, and at that they are only fifteen mages. Above that there is no referencing system so it is not said how many there actually are. There could be none just like there could be many.

Back to my practice of the spell, I've been trying to get a few hairs to be the colour Eliya used to have but for some reason I'm still not getting it right. I'll try a few more times and then I'm going to need to practise invocation magic. I left a few things in place I can remember to see if I can transport them to me. As I start the casting of the changing spell, I feel my fox friend try to talk to me. *Roarn I'm coming to see you. I miss you.* That's really sweet of her, I hope I have something nice to share in my lunchbox. Before she gets here, I start casting the spell I've been practising again and just as I'm about to modulate it so that it changes only hair colour, I feel my power ebb quite substantially. *Sorry, I think I just took your magic, I did not know I could do that. I'm almost there but it's hard to walk now, my body feels strange.* Says my fox friend. I would have thought that only Eliya can take magic from someone but it would appear that little vixen can take my spell or at least its wording. Not that a human changing spell would work on a fox, or at least I don't think so. It's not like I've been doing this for a long time and the time I've had did not make me a Master. The only thing is, according to my marks I'm at less than a fifth of my energy so I'll have to regenerate.

I'm about to sit down to rest and have some food when a very strange creature walks out from behind a tree. It's a naked girl, or young women I should say, but she has the ears and tail of a fox. Her fur is the usual orange colour of foxes but on her tummy it's white and her tail is tipped in white at well as her ears. Her skin looks as white as snow which is quite a strong contrast with the rest of her. I can see her feet hurt as she is having a hard time walking and that's when I realize that I'm staring. I look away, take off my jacket, and looking at the floor I walk up to her and cove her up.

- 'Are you lost?' That's the first thing I think of asking. Not what the heck are you or something logical, I'm more worried she is going to be cold or that she is lost. I asked in E'rtkinian hoping that the creature before me understands that.
- 'No Roarn I was coming right to you. What happened to my body is completely out of the realm of my understanding, though.' Wait, this is my fox friend. But what the hack happened to her. There is no way that I could have cast a spell strong enough to change her into a semi-human and yet that seems to be what happened.
- 'But how on earth did you end up changing like this? And are you cold my dear vixen?

- I think I stole your spell because it sounded right, it sounded like it would make me more like you and Eliya. Maybe this way I can be with you more often, I'm lonely here. And yes, I am cold, do you have somewhere warm to go? Without my fur the wind is cold.
- Wait. Are you telling me you wanted to be human? Why? You are such a beautiful vixen. And what can I call you?
- I'm lonely here, the packs don't want me so I'm always alone. If I'm human, I could at least make friends. And thank you for saying I'm beautiful. As for a name, may I look in your mind for one? I have no idea what a name for me should be.' So, she felt so lonely that she wanted to change out of being a fox just so that she could have company. That's actually really sad.
- 'I'll carry you I just need to pack up my stuff. We can go to my car and then to my parent's place. There is lots of space there and also there are other animals. Are you hungry?
- Nope, I had a pigeon not long ago. If you have something you want to share that would be nice though. And you did not say for the name.
- Yes little fox, look for what you need while I pack away my things.
- Thank you Roarn.'

As I pack up all my books and other bits and bobs, I take out some dried meat and a bag of dried fruit while listing all the girl names I can think of in my mind. 'Elfe' is all she says while I finish packing up. I give her my backpack and she puts it on her back before climbing onto my back. Considering the weight of my bag, she can't possibly weigh more than thirty or thirty-five kilograms. I give her some of my dried meat and she immediately eats it up before giving out a tiny little burp. I offer the dried fruit, and she tries a few before actually accepting. As I carry her through the forest towards the road, I start to hear other people and wonder if I should not cover her a little more. We near the parking and I see that there are only a few people so I hurry to my car and lower her into the passenger seat before going round to the driver side. The people present are so focused on their conversation that they don't even see us. I start the car and we are off.

- 'Have you decided what name you want to have?
- Yes, I want to be called 'Elfe', it sounds right. I've got pointy ears, I'm small, I'm fast and, according to you, I'm pretty.
- That is a good choice I guess, it's not a common name either so it suits you well as you are not a common creature.
- What do you think I am? I mean I'm still a fox, I think.
- I think you are more human than you think. I don't know how much energy I have but you used nearly all of

it, I had nine full lines left and I'm down to one and a half. Whatever you changed with my spell, you used a lot more energy than what small changes use.

- Oh, I'm sorry, I did not realize I was using your strength not my own. Will your parents not mind me? I mean I don't exactly look like you humans.
- I don't think so; they are still getting used to the fact that I can do magic but no one would be mean to a cute little elf.
- You're being nice to me again. It's strange. Why do you always say such nice things to me?
- Because you're my friend little elf and that is a good enough reason.
- I'm your friend? Really? I have a friend? Waou!' She is going half crazy to the point where her tail is wagging like crazy, thumping against the car seat.
- 'Yes Elfe, you are my friend.'

That's about the last thing we get to say before getting to my place and needing to hurry in before all the passing cars see her crazy wagging tail. It's not that she is not adorable but it's not exactly very discreet when I'm trying to get her into the house without being noticed.

Once inside and out the back she immediately starts sniffing around, falls over backwards and lies on the grass. *It smells like you here, I like it. Just wondering, do I have to keep this itchy thing on? It's really not comfortable.* The itchy thing being the only piece of clothing hiding her quite feminine lines and clear markings of her gender, well yeah, I guess I could give her something better. *Come up to my room we'll give you some better clothing.* We go up to my room, still no sign of my parents thankfully, I close my door and start to rummage through my stuff to find some small enough clothing for her. She is so tiny it's hard to find anything that would fit but I give her a pair of boxers, a pair of small shorts and a thin cotton shirt. With everything made of natural elements, it should not itch her too badly; or at least I hope not.

I don't even have time to turn around to give her some privacy that she is stripped down and trying to figure out how the clothing works. 'Please help me. I don't understand this stuff. It's strange fake fur.' She may seem my age I need to remember she has the mind of a fox not a human. I help her into the clothing, trying as much as possible not to look at the diverse parts of her anatomy she is clearly not trying to hide. It's quite a task to get the shorts on after the boxers as she has a huge fluffy tail that needs to come through somewhere. I end up cutting a little hole in the back of the shorts and giving her a belt to wear keeping the shorts up. She looks really small and fragile in my far too large clothing. I think out to Eliya over our mental link and tell her all that happened. She first laughs and then tells me she'll reach out to Master Oska and tell her what happened.

I invite Elfe to come down to meet my parents and visit my garden. She is probably going to stay like she currently is for a long time if not forever so I'd better get her a place where she can be herself. 'Roarn, do you mind me being like this? Or am I too strange?' Her mind sounds so sad I just give her a hug. And that's when she does something I'm really not expecting, she kisses me. Not a normal human type kiss, more like a huge lick across my lips. It's not a horrible feeling it just feels like a bad idea. 'You're not really supposed to do that Elfe. It means a lot between humans and only Eliya is allowed to do that to me. And to answer your question no, I find you look really sweet and I like you just as you are.' If truth be told, I find her absolutely adorable and want to play with her fur and ears. The only thing is, that may mean something totally different to a fox's mind so, I would rather not risk causing her discomfort.

- 'Come little one, lets have you meet my parents, they don't speak E'rtkinian but they will understand it and I'll translate their answers for you.' I walk her up the garden path to see where my parents are and we find them in deep discussion about my tutoring in magic with Master Oska.
- 'Greetings' Master,' I say with a slight bow. 'Mum and Dad, I would like you to meet Elfe, my vixen friend.' I let Elfe walk out from behind me and show herself.

- 'Hello.' She says with a very shy little voice, in E'rtkinian. Clearly, she is not used to being looked at so much because even Master seems gobsmacked.
- 'Why hello little fox, fancy seeing you again; and in a different form it would seem. I believe you two will have lots of explaining to do and Roarn you need to rest your energy is very low.' Says Master pointing at my marks that are only faintly coloured implying there is very little magic energy left in me.
- 'I will explain it all in depth later, for now I'm going to let Elfe visit the garden and then I will sleep a bit. Eliya will come soon as far as I know.
- That's good we need to speak a bit; we are going to the capital next week. No choice but to take time off, the matter is urgent. I'm sorting out all the complicated bits and bobs so don't worry. Go visit what you want to and we will discuss it all later.
- Thank you, Master.'

I take Elfe's hand/paw and we go towards the back of the garden and then field beyond it. She looks at me, smiles and takes off her shorts before running off into the field. It's more of a pasture than a field but it's really sweet to see her so playful. I go get a volley ball and we mess around a bit. *I have to say, I really do think I should be jealous but you two are far too adorable for that. Now I want a kiss so move it.* Comes Eliya's voice in my mind. I dash to the garage but Elfe beats me there and gives Eliya a hug and licks her mouth. I guess that is her version of a happy greeting. *Is she supposed to look nearly like a human? And why is she wearing so little?* I explain the whole series of events to Eliya and Master Oska who pitched up at the right time. My parents get a slightly less detailed version but they get the idea quite well and offer for Elfe to stay at our house. *She seems to really like you a lot, as in enough that I feel I should be jealous. Maybe we should ask Master how she could have taken that spell from you and used it on herself.* Eliya sounds a little angry but all together it's all going down a lot better than I had expected.

- 'With Elfe and the dangers for Eliya not to have her marks I have moved the day of our trips to next Tuesday. We will travel by portal to as close as we can to the city and then we get a ride in. I've sorted it all out with your work and university and everything. Also, Elfe is coming with us.' Says Master after all the explanations are done.
- 'How long are we going for? I mean I can't exactly miss more than two or three days of work.' Asks Eliya.
- 'We are going for two days and that includes travel time. We don't have time to go any longer, not for the moment at least.
- Are we supposed to take anything with us? Clothing, food, anything?

- No, just your brains and a full dose of energy, you're going to have to go past the academy, it's an obligation for any non-tested mage who enters the city. The only thing is, if they give you a space at the academy you would do well to take them up on their offer as that does not happen often.
- What does it imply? To go to the academy?
- Not much more than your university like you know it but something a little more magical too. You'll see when you go. It's a nice place I'll tell you that much.
- That's not exactly very precise. I suppose we have to take your word for it and wait.'

And that's pretty much what we do. Eliya and I spend as much time as possible learning all we can from the various codices we have not yet finished. Elfe spends most of her time learning the basics as she seems to be able to do magic too now that she is half human. It's quite fun to see her trying to first figure out why we would want to cast magic that makes us smell like rabbits. Just to make fun of her, I cast that spell and for three full hours I smell like a rabbit. The only snag with doing so is that, for those few hours, Elfe wanted to eat me. She tried only a few times and stopped at a lick across the face before blushing and turning away. I'm starting to wonder how much of her thoughts I can read and how much of mine she can. I would love to know what the real reason for her blushing is because I doubt it has to do with her so-called habit. She told me that licking others was a form of greeting to foxes and had no link to love or marking territory, that's now somewhat hard to believe.

Apart from messing about, we've been taking shifts sleep learning and speed learning as much as possible in anticipation to testing for the academy. We have just finished modifying a load of warm clothing and some other things. Eliya gave Elfe some clothing, girl clothing this time, and we spent some time modifying them to her interesting physique. And just so that you get some more juicy details I should tell you a few funny things. It took both Eliya and myself to force Elfe to take a shower. She hated the idea until we actually got her under a warm stream of water, then she started fox purring. Ever since then, she has wanted to shower with Eliya and I each time. That happened only once in the past days and it was a great test on what Elfe knew about male human bodies. She was surprised to see that we don't look the same between girls and boys. We laughed at that one and asked her if foxes and vixens look the same. Then she laughed and said that any fox who ever tried to get near her she would bite so she did not know what they looked like in comparison to her.

Other than that, well, we've been learning that my energy refills itself each time I cast a transportation spell or an invocation one. In other words, if I don't have time to rest, I need to use my elemental magic, thus invoke things. I've figured out how to do objects, it's just complicated when I need to put them back. To invoke, I think of where they are, what they are and how they look; with all that pictured out in my mind, I need to figuratively reach into the picture and pick out the object. The problem is if it has moved at all then I can't get it and I can't invoke things that are not mine in some way. I also don't know how big I can go but for now I've invoked my entire cupboard from one side to another of my house and back again. I can't invoke any other animal than Elfe and I can't move humans around at all.

On the morning of leaving for the capital, Antartis, Master Oska arrived at my parent's place a bit early, got a coffee and is now giving us a crash course in portaling. I was wondering why we had not yet learnt how to use portals and her reply is quite straight forward: only E'rtkin were allowed to create portals until two days ago. They changed the millennia old laws to allow for new magic students to use portals. The reason for this change is that there was far too much loss of power on the E'rtkin front against humans. The balance being in peril on levels hardly seen before they need all of us students to be ready to tutor new students within the next two years.

Eliya and Elfe are managing quite well with the portals, mine are apparently strange. Instead of going from one to another, my portals go into a void space and open up anyplace I can think of. If I understand it well, I'll never be able to use most of the portal magic but my portals can take me anywhere. The only thing is, no one else can use them. I only need to open one and enter. Then the exit, I open from within the void. There are quite a few constraints on this power though, I have to cast my entering portal against a surface, I can't cast in thin air like the others. Of course, the fact that I don't need to tunnel cast helps but it is still complicated.

We don't have more than an hour to practise before Master says it's time to go and conjures up the portal tunnel to the capital access area. We hop through and are immediately hit by a freezing breeze; it must be deadly for mages coming from a tropical area. It's not so much the climate change that is violent and painful, it's the light. The snow reflects all the sunlight like a deadly laser beam trying to burn out our retinas. We are ushered into a large glass building that was totally invisible just a second ago.

- 'Welcome Master Oska and AMO Roarn, AMO Eliya, Elfe. I, Grif'kin, will be your driver to the capital.' Says a middle aged, totally normal looking man. I was expecting it to be a dragon or something; meanwhile, it's just a normal person.
- 'Thank you Grif'kin, when do we leave?' Asks Master very politely.
- 'Right now, we are not expecting anyone else. Please get into the vehicle and be sure to remain seated for the

entire trip. You probably will not even see it happen.'
Smiles Grif'kin and leads us into a sleigh like train thing.
- 'Is this thing at least safe?' Asks Eliya.
- 'It's at least ten times safer than any other vehicle you
ever used in your life up until now.' Replies Grif'kin.

Next thing we know, the sleighmobile has departed at full speed. It's just as he said, too fast to see what is happening. Although, I would have liked to see what is outside, even if it is all snow and rock, the moment we break out of the freezing cold and reach the city-capital. I did not feel us breach the magical barriers so I suppose they are too powerful for apprentice mages to feel. Well now, enough of that let me tell you what an E'rtkin city looks like. The capital city actually.

Contrary to logic or fantasy, the city itself is very sober compared to some human cities like London and Paris. The only thing is that this soberness is clearly not the real face of the city. As our sleigh gets into a sort of station, I realize just how much of this city one could miss. The first thing is that the huge glass structures that form the perimeter of the city, actually reach up all the way to over the top of the city where they join. There is a huge hanging tear, as clear as the rest of the structures, floating over the middle of the city. I don't understand how any of that is actually staying up there but it is. As for the roads and houses, they are all different. Each climate on earth is represented in one way or another; be it the hot deserts or the frozen northern tundra, each one separated from the other by some form of magic. And more than those obvious bits of amazement made of glass, everything here seems to grow. It looks like nothing I've ever seen before, the houses and buildings seem to have been grown out of the elements themselves. There is no mortar and nothing looks blocky or angular; everything is made as single unites and perfectly united pieces. As much as I would like to continue these descriptions they are going to have to wait, an official has come to take us to the academy.

The Academy

Once on our way to the actual academy I realize just how amazing this place really is on a magical plane. There is no ice or snow on the roads, the roads themselves are cast from crystal and have what I guess to be lava under them. The heated paths and light given off by this structure is fairylike and quite something to see. If I could draw, I would put a sketch of it in here; it would be worth it.

We pass a lot of onlookers, all staring at us with wonder, fear or anger, and many children all with their marks visible on their arms. It would seem that marks are a form of recognition here; and if that is the case, it would explain why they are looking wearily at Eliya and Elfe. Elfe did not bother to cover her strangeness and thus is attracting a lot of attention to our group but it does not matter because we are at the academy within the minute.

The building itself is constructed from hundreds of interlocking pieces of different stone, wood and other elements I don't recognize. We are ushered in too fast for me to see any more details about the building but the entry hall is so surprising I almost fall over. Sitting in the hall, as if totally normal, completely still yet clearly alive, is a large dragon. I would never have thought I would come across a creature of legend like this one in my entire life but here it is. As we enter it opens an eye and looks at our group. *Greetings invoker, welcome to the academy and please stop being afraid I'm still small compared to my parents. I don't like the smell of fear. Give my greetings to Master Oska, Apprentice Eliya and your companion. By the may her name is not Elfe but E'ls'trint.* Comes the booming mental voice of the dragon into my mind. I repeat his words to Master and Eliya and then mentally ask Elfe what name she wishes to go by. Her reply is basically 'as long as you call me, I'll be happy' so that settles it, I'll use her real name.

'Greetings Master Oska, Apprentice Eliya, Apprentice Roarn, Apprentice Companion E'ls'trint. Welcome to the academy of Antartis, please follow me.' Says a very official looking man who appeared in the room only a second before. He does not wait for us to reply and immediately walks off into a corridor to the side of the hall and then into a room. We follow him in silence and when he gestures for us to sit in the room we do.

- 'Good day Professor T'erinkl, thank you for seeing us. You already know who this lot is, will you be doing their tests?' Says Master as if it's totally normal that we had to wait to be in his office before talking and all that.
- 'Yes Oska, I know who they are, their magic has reached me and no it will not be me.' Replies the professor.

- 'It will be me that shall do their tests and who shall decide to let them join the academy. But before that I'm going to give Eliya her marks. She can't absorb my magic.' Says another person after just appearing in the room as if it's normal, I guess it is. This time she is dressed perfectly normally, on E'rtkin standards, so not much decoration. Yes, a woman, she is about 1m70 tall and has extremely long white hair. She's probably what you would think an elf looks like.

- 'I do not remember you from my time at the academy, who are you, Miss?' Asks Master Oska quite surprised that this person would but in like that. Clearly, the professor must be very important if she is so taken aback by someone daring to chirp in when he talks.

- 'You would not know me Master Oska, I was off planet when you were here. My name is Lily Lightwind, mythical tier mage of teleportation and space warping.' Oh well that would explain why she just appeared out of thin air, but what the heck, mythical tier. I would not have thought to even meet one in my life. Also, what does off-planet mean?

- 'My apologies Mrs Lightwind. How did the mission go in the end?

- No need to apologize Oska and please, call me Lily. The mission went very well thank you, the sanctuary is ready for use. Now back to your students will each of you please stand and present yourselves to me.' She looks at us expectingly so I stand and say my name. I've no idea what she wants to know other than that.

- 'Presenting oneself to an E'rtkin means more than just your name Roarn, you need to show your marks.' Says Master. I do as I'm told and show her my forearms. She smiles and touches them with the tip of a stone she conjured up. My marks change a little, they broaden and seem to gain in detail.

- 'Thank you Roarn, I'll test you in a few minutes. E'ls'trint, you're next, I need to give Eliya her marks before I can do anything.' She looks at E'ls'trint and then at me. 'Oh, I did not realize you are his familiar, may I give her marks Roarn? It will make her even more bonded to you.' I had no idea she could have marks.

- 'Yes Mrs Lightwind, you may if she agrees.' *You don't have to accept little fox.* I say to the mage and then to my fox friend.

- 'I would like marks please.' Interjects E'ls'trint.

- 'Then take my hand, and you two Eliya. We will be back in a few minutes.'

The Mythical mage takes their hands and disappears taking them with her. Again, I'm wondering how on earth it's possible for her to teleport around in this city that is supposed to be protected from those sorts of things. The more I think of it the more I wonder how it's even possible to be as powerful as she must be. Seriously, she is respected as if she were royalty.

- 'Master, what is the sanctuary?' It's been bothering me for a while now to have no idea what they are talking about. I know I'm still learning magic and all that but it seems a bit huge not to know a thing about it.
- 'It's an off-planet mission called the sanctuary. The project is happening on the moon and on the red planet. Fifteen of the most powerful mages are joining their magic to make two sanctuaries for all the living species on earth. Meaning all animals and all plants. It's an effort to preserve all life forms.
- How on earth can they set those sorts of things up on the moon and on Mars? Is it not impossible to live there?
- Not with the right kinds of magic and a lot of effort and time. The mission has been going on for nearly two hundred years.
- So, it's now possible to live on Mars and the moon?
- Only in the sanctuaries but yes, especially Mars, their effort has truly paid off there.
- Well now, that I would like to see one day.
- Then you better work hard and hope your potential magic level is at least Mythical level. Ah, here they come.'

How she knows they are on their way back considering that they are teleporting, I have no idea. But she is right, a second later the three reappear out of thin air like they left. Eliya has her arms absolutely covered in marks. All the burn scars she had are now traced in gold and blue lines. E'ls'trint has exactly the same marks as me on her arms and she also has quite a large disk tattoo on her belly and a similar one on her back. They are large and very complex circles interlocked in a fancy way. Mrs Lightwind comes up to me and without a word touches my back as well. I feel very little contrary to my marking but I know that I now have a clone of E'ls'trint's mark on my back. The moment that is done I feel something absolutely weird happen; you know that horrible feeling you have when you have a burp that does not want to come out and then it does, well it's like that. *Roarn, did you feel that? It was as if something really big was blocking my mind and is now gone.* Well, at least I was not alone feeling it, that's reassuring. *Yes E'ls'trint, I did feel it and it was strange. I'm going to inquire about it.*

Well, I would have liked to but I don't have the time because, before I know it, we are being teleported somewhere else. I blink and we are in a huge room filled with a lot of people, as in hundreds of people. It is some sort of amphitheatre and it would seem as if a large part of the city's population is here. I was hoping that the testing was a very private and restrictive thing; meanwhile a few hundred people are going to see it happen.

'Abiding by the laws of our people, these apprentice mages will be tested before the people of Antartis. They are two human youths and a vixen who chose to become like one of us.' Comes a booming voice in the amphitheatre. E'ls'trint attracts a lot of attention but then so do Eliya and myself. 'They shall be tested my Mythical Mage Lily Lightwind and if they are powerful and able enough, they will be tutored here at the high academy of E'rtkin magic.' Continues the powerful voice.

'Step forth Roarn, you shall go first as the girl's marks need to impregnate a little more.' I walk up to Mrs Lightwind and she has me sign a huge scroll of paper and cast a spell that copies my marks onto it. When that is done, I have to swear an oath in E'rtkinian and then only does the testing start. My first and apparently only task is quite basic in naming but horribly hard in practice. I am to fuse, modulate and cast the most powerful spell my energy will allow me to. I have no idea what my energy is worth and how much I have so I first cast a measuring spell and when the digits appear in front of me there is a general gasp in the crowd. I guess that means it's either really good or really bad; to me it just says 12,145,343. That's a really big number but still it's not as if I can teleport around like my examiner or throw hundreds of portals like Master Oska.

Next, I invoke my personal notes on the spells I learnt and see why there was a large gasp, my energy reading should allow me to cast nearly Master tier magic. If I at least knew such spells, of course. I don't bother reading the spells themselves, it's just the energy readings I want to see. Once I find a spell that uses a few hundred thousand units of energy I look at its function, it alters the essence of one's energy into mater or another kind of energy. That will do.

I walk to the middle of the amphitheatre, followed closely by E'ls'trint and the examiner. In that place I start thinking out the wording and then start casting my spell. It goes something like this: 'May my energy part from my being in sufficient amount to leave me standing, then let it fuse with the air around me altering its core value to that of carbon in twelve percent, silver in twenty-eight percent and gold in fifty-five percent, then as much as is needed must force the carbon to heat and compress.' I start. It takes a toll but I see that I still have two and a half lines left on my marks even if they are glowing less brightly. When I have in front of me a pile of diamond dust, a pile of silver dust and a large pile of gold dust people start clapping. *You can do this Roarn, I believe in you.* Says Eliya in my mind. *You will manage this master.* Says E'ls'trint as well. Then I continue my casting: 'The matter before me, fuse, join on a level unseen until you become the shape I have in my mind. Alter your energetic signature until you are marked to mine. Eliminate all of your impurities and become as pure as needed for your function.' The toll this time is a lot less than I would have expected even if the spell I'm using is out of no book but rather a command infused with my magical energy.

The image I had in mind was that of a royal ornamental dagger, the only thing is that I accidentally inverted the elements and made the blade of diamond and the stonework be shaped bits of gold. The silver is used to hold the elements of the dagger together. In the end the result is pretty awesome and I still have a half line of energy left so I'm fine. It's going to take a few days to sleep this one off, I think, but that's okay.

'Are you finished Roarn?' Asks Mrs Lightwind. I nod, she takes the dagger and inspects it then casts a few spells and it is projected holographically enlarged above us so that all can see it. She then tries its edge and finds it totally useless, it's as sharp as a stick. She then hands it to E'ls'trint how tests the edge on a piece of wood and the blade cuts straight through it. 'As you can see, people of Antartis, not only did he create a magnificent blade out of his own energy but he also made is useable by only those who bear the mark of his energy. I shall take your vote for his entering of the academy and then we shall classify his magic.' There is clapping and then silence. A few seconds later I see a diagram in mid-air that is half full of green and half full of blue. It then blurs before ending up with a lot of green and very little blue.

'Roarn is thus accepted to join the high academy of magic of Antartis with an 89 percent majority. I shall now cast the testing spells to rate his current magic power, his potential magic power and his magic type.' Says Lily Lightwind. She then starts chanting and the crowd echo her words at full voice. Whatever they are casting it is powerful enough to make the place crackle with energy. Well, everywhere apart from around Eliya who is absorbing it. Then next thing I know I'm lying on the ground and I can hear Eliya casting what I suppose is her exam spell. I get up and try to understand what she is doing and what is happening.

I don't get much of what her spell is supposed to do but she is clearly not caring in the slightest about the energy level she uses. Whatever the result is going to be it is sure to be impressive. Not quite legendary level but I would not be surprised if she creates something totally crazy powerful.

I have to wait quite some time before I know what she is making and, in that time, E'ls'trint comes up to me and licks me across the face before nibbling my ear. Just as she is playing miss adorable, I start to wonder what on earth happened while I was out. 'I created a scabbard for the dagger you made using a spell like yours. Thus, I am also accepted into the academy. As for the rest, we have to wait for the results they will tell us when Eliya is done with her test.' Well, that's almost not surprising that they would wait, especially considering I went and passed out on them. Second time that has happened, it's starting not to be fun.

After what seems like forever, Eliya finishes her casting and at first, I see nothing and then she says one word 'execute'. Just then a storm builds above her, thankfully this place does not have a roof, the storm grows in power but stays small and then a single bolt of lightning comes down straight at her. I hear people shout out in fear but strangely the electricity slows down and comes to a halt above her head. She reaches out, touches the tip of it and the energy disappears leaving behind it a huge pillar of clear glass that then goes all the shades of the rainbow before shattering into hundreds of little marbles. She lets out another command and the marbles role, one to each person in the crowd. The people pick them up and applause break out. I clap too but before long the voting takes place and Eliya gets a 98 percent 'yes' to enter the academy. Ten percent more than me, I could almost be jealous if her magic was not so amazing.

Mrs Lightwind starts the classification chant and is joined by all but Eliya, so including me. I feel the spell draw a tiny bit of my energy but it's hardly noticeable.

'I shall now give the results for Eliya, E'ls'trint and Roarn, students of the Antartis Academy of Magic.' Starts Mrs Lily Lightwind. 'Eliya Raven is to be classified as a Top Tier mage with Legendary potential. E'ls'trint is to be classified as a High tier mage, Master familiar and has Mythical potential. Roarn Rogue is to be classified as a Top Tier mage with Legendary potential.' She smiles at us and then repeats her words without the voice amplification but imbuing them with magic. My marks shift a little and so do those of Eliya and E'ls'trint. We then wait for the next bit, the part that tells us officially what elements we are. 'Eliya Raven is of three elements, electricity, rock and light. E'ls'trint is of fire and plant elements. Roarn Rogue is of four elements: void, pure energy, alteration and something we do not have a name for. He has the ability to mutate human technology into E'rtkin magical devices. Or at least we think so.' She lets that hang for a while before pulling out a cell phone and handing it to me before telling me to let my element take over and do the work.

After a few minutes of expectation and the crowd getting bored, I actually understand what she meant. I channel some energy into the cell phone and that's when the thing goes all crazy and starts buzzing and I don't know what. Mrs Lightwind smiles and lifts up her hand showing me the phone's battery. I'm using magic to power the thing. And not only that, it's somehow learning a load of stuff from me. I try to focus on making the phone able to call and have internet connection and somehow it actually seems to understand. In other words, I have to mentally focus the magic and it does the rest. Or at least that works for now, it will probably become a lot trickier in time and with more complex bits of technology.

After general astonishment at all those announcements, we are spirited away back into the office of Mr T'erinkl where our parents are somehow waiting for us.

Inscribing in the Academy

To say the least, I was not expecting to see my parents here, not even vaguely. I mean let's be honest, I hardly told them anything about the whole magic life and E'rtkin history. About how humans are almost a dirty version of E'rtkin people and all that. It's always better to stay safe rather than be sorry, well now I'm sorry. In the very basic looking office sit our parents, looking at us expectantly and with a glimmer of wonder.

- 'We invited your parents to come and see your testing ceremony and thus gave them authorization to regularly visit you here. A portal gate shall be set up for you all.' Starts the professor.
- 'As for your inscriptions, I will need you three to go and change into these.' Says Mrs Lightwind handing us each a very thin soft robe and a simple pair of boxer short type underwear. She also gives the girls bandana looking things to support their lady parts. 'Hurry now you have class in half an hour and we need to do the paperwork. There is an empty room next door on the right.'
- 'They are already starting class? But how about their university courses?' Asks mum.

- 'They will spend a month and a half in full boarding school here, catching up nearly fifteen years of classes that they missed. Then we will make it an on and off thing until their university year is done and as soon as that is over it will be nonstop academy till the next university year.' Answers Master Oska before shoving us out the room.

We find the empty room, walk in and check it's really empty. Then, between the three of us we conjure up all the necessary things to get clean in twenty seconds flat. How about a spell that makes a shower be an instant cleaning thing, and then creates the shower out of the humidity in the air? Well, that's what we end up doing and then a nice pine and rosemary perfume we cast on each other before getting dressed again. Yes, that does mean that we were all three naked in the same room so stop getting perverted idea readers!

As we enter the office again, I can see why the paperwork could have been a problem, there are quite a lot of stacks of papers and they all look annoying to fill in. Thus, we get cracking as fast as we can and fill in all the normal details, imprint our marks on at least four places and even leave a drop of blood on one of them. It immediately brings up our full-blood spectrum and purity level. The amount of information they need is at first scary but when I realize what it adds up to, I understand better. If one is to cast a spell that takes too much energy then it consumes your innate energy until there is only dust left of you. The thing is, if the people you are with are aware of your natural necessities they can heal you faster than you deteriorate and thus save your life. For that to work, they need to know as much as possible about you and that includes full-body mass index and blood spectrum.

For the hostel forms, we even have to say how we would prefer to stay and, in the end, we go for a double room with an adjoining bathroom rather than separate suites each. That makes our parents screech their teeth until I remind them that Eliya and I are engaged and are already living together in the human world. That's when they come back to their senses and remember that we are also officially adults. 'Well, actually, with the life expectancy of the E'rtkin you two are still children for another two and a half years for Eliya and nearly five years for Roarn.' Interjects the professor giving our parents a few points of credibility.

Once all the paperwork is done, the professor tells us he'll be one of our main tutors and that Master Oska will be going to recruit at least another five or six apprentices. That being done, we walk out and go towards the dorms.

The dormitory of the Academy is a joined building that is separated into a lot of different bits. It's almost like a pile of dominoes that went wrong and someone just added rooms and doors. There is no question of separation of gender or age; what creates the groups here is elemental affinity and power level. You are always placed with people who do not have the same elements as you and who are either much more or much less powerful. In those groups the genders are separated by magic not rules; if you prefer, it's impossible for couple things to happen if you don't have an authorisation to do so. Those come in at a later age of eighteen at minimum and are quite strictly regulated. The other separations are set in by age but in a strange way. Rather than be set up in a splitting way it's set by large age groups. From six to twelve is one group, then twelve to eighteen and lastly eighteen to twenty-four. The last year being done outside of the academy.

We get to our room on the twelfth floor of the 'spirit' building. It's placed in direct view of the academy grounds and training centre and has a lovely view outside of the city and into the ice-covered reaches beyond. It's certainly one of the most beautiful places I've ever been in the room domain. The doorway is magically bound to us three and needs us to actually name our visitors for them to enter. And that's only the door.

Once open and each person 'invited' in, we have time to look around for about two minutes before having to go to class. We step into the room and I immediately feel it's special. How they got it to be like this in just the few hours that went past for our testing and inscription, probably a lot of magic.

Against the far wall is a huge window space looking out, as I said, to the academy grounds and Antarctica beyond. The ceiling is covered in plant and growth, the floor is made of large rocks, grass and soft moss. The walls look like a forest and the entire place smells exactly like the dark parts of a forest. They really did a beautiful job of making this place for us and I can't begin to fathom how hard it must have been to modulate it all for us in such a short time.

There is a table made out of a seemingly growing tree and the chairs are bent roots. The lighting is for us to do, and the food is in common with the rest of our building down in the dining hall. We don't have time to visit the room before we are ushered off to our first class of the day. It's actually one of the last classes given today but we still have to go. It's forbidden to miss a single class at the academy, unless if one has a high-level excuse pass given only by the head of the academy. In all other cases, the punishment for absence is a crescendo from attending five extra hours of class to being expelled forever from the academy. As magical education is an obligation, if one is expelled then you have to go to one of the other academies and some don't even accept previously expelled students.

Well, enough of that, it's time for our first class.

Our first class

Entering the classroom discreetly was supposed to be mission number one, that failed. Getting a seat without being noticed: failed. Trying not to look dead shy and scared and wonder-struck: failed. Well, the bit we did manage was to get three seats next to each other. A minute later Mrs Lily Lightwind walks in and greets the class. I hear a load of my fellow students gasp in wonder and some even clap before the mythical mage lifts a hand and silences the class. We are nearly two hundred in the amphitheatre-like room and all fall dead silent when she starts talking.

'As you all realized, and most witnessed their testing, we have three new students in the academy as of today. I expect you to welcome them warmly as you are now peers and to guide them in their first days here. Also, I shall be seeing a bit of you while I'm here as I teach evolving energy magic. I shall thus be teaching you how to make your energy or an energy you control mutate over time and as such be less demanding on your bodies and minds to cast.' Her voice reaches all parts of the amphitheatre clearly showing that the acoustics of this place are surprisingly powerful. She continues about the description of the type of magic and I make sure my brain is set to full remember mode because, of course, we forgot to bring anything to take notes on. The other students have strange slates that look like tablets and are running their fingers of them like a keyboard but faster. I see some have diagrams show up and one student is directly drawing on her tablet thingy. I wonder where they got those, I'll have to ask. *Master, I need to go do my foxy business, do you think I can do so?* Asks E'ls'trint in my mind. Why she calls me master I don't know but what I'm quite sure of is that she should probably not bother the teacher by leaving class. *I really can't wait too much longer, please send me off and invoke me after or something. I don't want to bother the teacher.* If only I knew how to do that properly. I visualize our room and picture E'ls'trint disappearing from here and then arriving there and to my surprise it actually works and demands almost no effort. *Thank you master, I'll tell you when I'm ready to come back.*

- 'Roarn Rogue, you are not supposed to use transportation magic in class unless if you ask. What was your reason for doing that?' Asks the professor.
- 'Excuse me Mrs Lightwind I did not know that. E'ls'trint had some personal business to attend to that could truly not wait and we did not want to bother your class.' I don't want to say that she had to go to the little girls' room but clearly the message got across quite well because the entire class laughs. *I'm ready to come back.*

Says my familiar. I reach out to her over that strange link that we have and use to talk and then call for her with my mind. A second later she pops out of the void and back into her seat.

- 'I see you are done with your business little fox; you would do well to know that it's perfectly allowed to go to the restroom during class and that it does not bother the professors at all.
- I'm sorry Mrs Lightwind I did not know that. I shall be careful from now on.
- Just a warning for now, but don't use transportation magic in class again alright.
- Yes ma'am.'

We settle back into our class and as it goes on, we learn all about the ways we can set our energy to move slower and thus not use energy to move energy. Also, I learn at least a few new words but clearly, I'm nowhere near the level of my classmates. Just the way some of them are taking their notes is proof enough of their higher knowledge of the language. Their tablets seem to have a form of auto-centring system that makes them always be in the middle of it. I really need to get my hands onto something like that but I'm not even sure how currency works in the E'rtkin world. They did not exactly explain that sort of thing when they brought us here as it was all a bit of a rush due to Eliya not having her marks.

I have no idea what the time is but what I soon figure out is that classes are quite long here and also quite tiring to follow as they contain a heck of a lot of information. I wonder if they realize that to us human students this feels like years of classes compressed into hours. I have no idea how we are supposed to catch up years of their classes in months if hours of classes feel like years. It's going to be a huge strain on our little brains and it's going to be tiring. You are probably thinking that it's all easy and basic if we can remember everything only by listening but to do that actually uses energy units at quite a pace, and I've not had time to rest since the testing thus I'm going to drop off soon. *I'll feed you some of my energy Master and then you can share the course back with me after class. It's supposedly possible, they told me I could after you passed out during your marks' ceremony.* She is so adorable; I wish I could hug her more often. *Oh, but you can Roarn just not in class and not too much you're my betrothed after all.* Says Eliya into my mind. I always forget that she can come and go from my thoughts as she wants. *I would be glad to have some energy my dear little fox, I'll be sure to give you all you may miss.* I reply to E'ls'trint.

We make it through class and at the end of class we are to go back to the dormitory and then go for dinner half an hour later. Outside, the sky is full of stars and the streets of the city are glowing from the lava lights under the streets. I still can't believe they use molten rock as a source of heat and light, that's just crazy. Once out in the corridor I realize that there must be a lot less restriction for magic once class is over because half the students are messing around with colouring each other's hair or clothing and then throwing around flotation magic thus making bags fly above their owners and girl's shirts lift slightly. I guess one does not need to be human to have pesky silly games.

When we arrive at the dormitory buildings, the groups separate and many hugs are exchanged saying good night. Eliya, E'ls'trint and I go off towards the Spirit building and find ourselves in a flow of students from our class. Some just say hi while others are being quite snob like and are making fun of my foxy. She bares her fangs at one of them and that seems to keep them calm for a few minutes. A boy comes up to us and starts a conversation.

- 'Hi, I'm T'il'kin, I'm the guardian student for our floors of the Spirit building. Welcome to the Academy and well done for your testing it was pretty amazing.' He's about Eliya's age if I'm to guess and seems to be quite athletic. Seeing the girls ogling him, he is also very popular.
- 'Nice to meet you T'il'kin, I guess you know our names. Thanks for actually greeting us, the others seem to not really appreciate us much for some reason.' Replies Eliya.
- 'That probably because you tested in at such a late age and such a high level and potential. Most of us have

been here since we were six of seven and started at base level with master or parliamentary potential. Few ever test in at the top tier and over twelve.' He smiles at a group of people who branch off to one of the other floors and says he'll see them at dinner.

- 'We did not exactly choose to get here so late, a few months ago we had no idea this place existed and E'ls'trint was just a normal vixen in a forest. Why would they be envious or annoyed about that?' Asks Eliya slightly aggravated.
- 'I know that but that's because I was briefed on your arrival and the conditions of it. It should be alright in any way, for now go do your ablutions and be ready in thirty minutes for dinner. I'll come and get you.' He waves us goodbye and goes to the other end of the corridor, leaving us here, in front of our door.

Back in our room our parents are waiting for us, that was quite unexpected. They simply tell us that they hopped home and brought us some personal things like my iPod and headphones and a few other things. We don't need any life necessities at the academy, they give us all we need as part of our schooling. Thus meaning that, all students wear the same uniforms and have the same type of accessories. The rules state that we are only allowed one or two personal accessories at all times.

Our parents are only allowed a short moment with us before they have to leave. We will be seeing them in a few days' time and for a few days at that due to the exam period. Once they are gone, we only have fifteen minutes to get ready for dinner and that means washing and changing.

E'ls'trint and Eliya take the bathroom first leaving me to pack our few belongings away and I get our clothing out. The wardrobe is full of uniforms on three different colour hangers, one for each of us. I take out three clean sets of clothes and set them at the ready by the bathroom and then go and perch myself in one of the branches to read. We have a very large stack of books to read so we'll be mentally sharing some of the information we learn but that does not mean we don't each have to read the entire pile of books. It was only about five books earlier on now it's nearly fifty. I hope it's not going to reach five hundred by tomorrow.

The girls leave me a five-minute window to get showered and ready and it's not exactly easy to achieve. The shower, or should I call it magically controlled waterfall is at exactly the temperature of my body and thus does not feel hot or cold of anything other than cleansing. All soap and shampoo are made following the basic necessities of one's body and thus smell quite interesting. Nothing unpleasant but a totally indescribable smell that is for sure. I manage to be ready when T'il'kin knocks on the door to guide us to the dining hall.

As we walk down the corridor, the rest of our floor join us and we are soon a full seventeen-member group walking towards the dining area of our building. Our guide explains a few things about the timing system and the reason everything is set like clockwork. There are very old spells in this place, as old as the founders of the academy, sometimes harmless but sometimes less so, and one can never be sure of what they might cause. He goes on to tell us about someone dropping dead due to one of these spells and then explains that they have been limited to certain times of day and night. Thus, as long as we are never late and not walking the corridors during unsafe times there should be no problem. I don't really believe him but it's good to be warned I suppose.

Once we are at the dining hall, I realize that, just like technology is common in the human world, so magic is here. I can hear hundreds of spells being cast, all minor ones, base magic and low tier at most, but so many. Actually, only when they stop do I realize just how many there were. Silence falls on the dining hall and then someone lets out a light gasp. That is the start of mayhem, what is only a few hundred but feels like millions of voices start speaking, shouting or laughing at once. *Roarn, why are they making fun of us?* Asks E'ls'trint in my mind. I receive so much of her feelings that I even feel her shiver. I turn to her, take her hand and just walk on forward. *I don't really know little fox but don't worry about them, let's just eat.*

On those words I feel a light gust of wind pass me and lift both Eliya and E'ls'trint's skirts. Just high enough to flash some upper thigh at the boys but that makes me want to punch the one who did that anyway. *Are they serious, let's just sit down and try to have dinner? Roarn, it's our first day, we are bound to attract attention.* Says Eliya with an annoyed but calm voice. *Master, may I bite the one who cast that spell?* Asks E'ls'trint right after. She can hear Eliya's words in mind since our bond broadened and I don't know how to cut her off yet. *Point him out to me first please.* She points to a younger age group student; he must be about sixteen and is grinning at his friends. He then sees E'ls pointing at him and mockingly bares his teeth at her. The wrong thing to do it would seem; she does not say a word but I feel her magic power take a tiny dip and there he is, his clothing changed into dry leaves that soon start to fall.

By the time he realizes what happened we are at the other end of the table and seated waiting for dinner to arrive. But before it does, there is a little amount of chaos as boywithleaves got angry and started to loudly cast a mid-tier spell at us. Some of the higher age group students are laughing, others are trying to warn us and lastly some are yelling for him to stop. It's forbidden to use anything above low tier magic without authorization in the academy. Pity for him, what E'ls'trint did to him was hardly base magic for her. It was just an elemental shift towards her element and that is ridiculously low magic, it does not even need wording as long as the elements are close. Cotton to dry cotton leaves is pretty easy in those conditions.

'Roarn, he is nearing the end of his spell and considering how long it was I think it's a lot more than one spell. I bet he accumulated about five or six spells into one to make it stronger.' Says Eliya out loud and quite obviously so that I'm not the only one to hear it. Boywithleaves says the last word of most spells 'k'rlin' that pretty much means 'execute command'. I see his marks glow a bit and then more than half of them blink out of colour. That spell is going to hurt and I have not yet learnt defensive magic.

'R'ifken neiyt.' Two words shouted in a voice full of liquid hatred, something I've never even felt before. It's as if the person who said them was intent on killing but holding himself or herself back. The voice was so drowned out but the wave of magic power that I could not even hear if it was a boy or a girl. The words are foreign to me but they are clearly powerful, the spell sent at E'ls'trint materializes and flickers out of existence in mid-air. Silence has covered the hall with its smothering blanket and it's broken only by a loud bang as food appears on all the tables.

- 'Do excuse my intruding, I'm quite sure you had the situation well covered but I could not bear to see your familiar shiver any longer.' Comes a soft voice behind me as I start dishing up Eliya, E'ls and myself.

- I turn and am face to face with a boy around my age looking at me sheepishly. 'Actually, I wish to thank you for intervening, you saved us from whatever that boy was sending our way.' I smile at him.

- 'It was a destruction spell aimed at your familiar's tail; it was going to rip it bare of its fur. I'm truly sorry for having intervened, though, it was out of turn of me.' He looks at his feet as if expecting an earful. E'ls shuffles closer to me and pats the bench next to her.

- 'Please join us mister, I'm very grateful you helped me out because it would have been really painful otherwise.' The tidal wave of joy that comes over our mental bond tells me just how happy she really is.

- 'May I Roarn?' He asks me. I nod and he takes the seat next to E'ls.

- 'Why are you constantly asking me for authorization and why are you saying sorry for having helped us?

- Even if there have not been any familiars in Antartis for a while, there are still laws on how to approach the situations where there are. It's strange to apply them in this case as your familiar looks like one of us but I was taught to do so anyway.

- And why don't you use her name?

- It's not legal to do so without your authorization or a hierarchical position that gives me the right.

- Please use my name, it's much nicer. And thank you very much for having helped me.' Says E'ls'trint smiling at him. She leans forward and kisses his cheek before grinning again.

Our conversation goes on for the rest of the meal and I learn many things about the various rules of the academy. One of which is that there will be no authority present other than that of the other students. We are to regulate each other into following the rules and thus if someone breaks one, his comrades are to punish him. I also learn that, even if the food we are getting looks really strange it's specifically made to be very nutritious and perfectly balanced. There are meat, vegetables and fruit in masses but for some reason when I've had enough, I just don't feel like more. The more we talk the more I realize just how much there is to learn about these people. It's not as if they are just other people on earth, they are an entire race of different. Their very way of thinking puts them in a totally different category to any of us humans and I need to learn to be as close as I can to that. I've been wondering a lot about how on earth it's going to work out with my parents and Eliya's but in the end that has little importance as we were bound to change at adulthood in any way. There is little anyone can do that will stop us from being our own person and a different one at that; diverging quite strongly from the teachings of human society.

When dinner is over Ad'emeiy, for that is his name, pulls out a flat piece of crystal and looks at me expectantly. I have no idea what he wants nor what the piece of crystal does but when I see his look change to surprise I understand that I'm missing out here. I tell him that I don't know what his crystal thingy is and he first laughs and then looks at me as if taken aback. 'It's a communicator, or what you would call a phone, you don't have one?' he says. I reply that I only have human tech and nothing E'rtkin for the moment, I don't even know what their currency is so I can't just go out and get one either. He promises to take us out and explain all those things on tomorrow's midday break and then bids us goodnight with a long look at E'ls making her blush. And of course, because of our bond I end up being a tomato face too; thanks, *E'ls'trint I love you too. It's my pleasure Master, love you lots as well.*

A Visit to the City

Our first night at the academy started really well and ended in a cuddle pile. Just as I was falling asleep next to Eliya, and E'ls'trint was already in her bed nest in the other room, I heard a tiny fox snore and knew she was out. Never had I heard her sleep so well. After having slept a bunch of hours, I felt some movement behind me and then a little arm wrap around me; E'ls had a nightmare and decided she wanted me as comfort. When I woke up, I had Eliya against my chest, in my arms and E'ls was in hers. They are both sleeping lightly and look absolutely adorable to the extent where I make my mind memorize the scene for a later memory.

We go for breakfast at eight in the morning with the rest of our floor and meet up with Ad'emeiy. He's planned us a whole two hours of distractions in the city and told us we must just ask our tutor before going out as they need to mark it down. He's already asked his and when I tell him I don't know who our tutor is he replies that it's the person who tested us into the academy. In other words, it's Lily Lightwind. We have a bunch of laughs when the guywearingleaves comes in and goes and sits on the far end of the hall to get away from us. We've made an enemy, probably even a few but too bad. Ad tells us that the free periods for our level are right after lunch and last an exact two hours. We are to be back on the academy grounds at exactly three o'clock and not a minute later. Apparently, the punishment for being late is an entire night of force learning; meaning you have to learn an entire codex in one night.

After breakfast we have physical magic class, I do not have the faintest idea what that is and so we just follow our classmates and hope for the best. Turns out physical magic is E'rtkin sport; it's about ten minutes of theory before we go out into the field and practice. We are learning what they call 'K'vif' a sort of martial art combined with base magic spell layering and a lot of weaponry. Of course, us three new students are at a great disadvantage and we lose all our sparing matches. Well, apart from E'ls who sucker punches her one opponent and knocks him out. Other than that, we lose everything and even more when it's the armed fights. The teacher takes note of this and gives us three voluminous codices to learn before our next session next week. I wonder how all of this is going to work out with all my human world stuff.

Being nicely bruised up, we head to the next class and, to my surprise, I hear a few classmates chanting together a healing spell and then healing Eliya, E'ls and myself. I thank them and ask if they need any healing and they all say that no they went unharmed. As we arrive at our next class, another one I don't know anything about, 'Preparation class', Mrs Lightwind calls us over to the side.

- 'I hear you lot want to go out later on, is that correct?' She asks with a smile.
- 'Yes Miss it is, we were told we need to ask you before we do so, though.' Replies Eliya.
- 'Well, yes you must and yes you may go, but first I'll need to see you briefly in my office. Try and finish lunch a little early and I'll be waiting for you. Oh, and avoid getting into any more trouble like yesterday.' She does not even wait for us to respond and just blinks out of being there.

So, the preparation class is one of the only non-magic classes we get here and it only lasts five sessions. We missed the first three. It's a bit like orientation class and it's to prepare us to choose our future jobs and also to teach us all the correct rules when speaking and meeting people of different ranks. Interestingly enough, there is no form of discrimination even if there is a form of ranking; instead, the curtesy just changes slightly. To someone of same of lower rank one is to greet by showing the marks of one arm and by promising a truthful conversation, with someone of higher rank or a foreigner it's to be both arms and the same promise. There is a certain amount of dress codes and things but, as the teacher says, none of them are obligatory. The only real lawful act we must all learn to do is the one of announcing. The E'rtkin always start an important conversation with an introductory sentence about the subject. For instance, if you want to talk about coffee then there is no need to announce it unless you are a professional but, if you want to talk about legendary tier magic, then you say: 'I wish to converse about legendary magic with thee' and then off goes the conversation.

After that class it's lunch time so we meet up with Ad'emeiy and have lunch together before we go off to see our tutor. He comes with us but waits in the corridor as we go to see her.

- 'I wish to converse about finances and education with the three of you.' She starts. 'As you just arrived in our world you don't yet know how our economy works nor do you have any of our utilities such as a communicator of a page crystal. So, I'll give you a quick crash course.'
- 'Is a page crystal the tablet things that our classmates have?' Asks Eliya.
- 'No, those are information crystals, you could get one too if you like. They are definitely in your price range.
- What currency do they use here?' I ask.
- 'We don't use money or anything like you are used to, we exchange energy or services for goods. And we have gratitude tokens that can be used to purchase energy from the central crystal banks.

- So, we just exchange energy for goods, is that not too easy? I mean we regenerate it daily.' Asks E'ls.
- 'That is why you often pay a lot, and also you need to remember that most things are doable with energy so, for those who have a lot, creating gold is easy therefore it has no value to us. Only energy is a source of wealth as it is what gets us around.' She looks at us and then bares her forearms so we can see her marks. They are fifteen lines of interlocking symbols.
- 'What do your marks say Miss?' Asks E'ls again.
- 'They are no longer just my marks; they contain all my credentials to access the sanctuaries and to breach the Antartis protections unharmed. Enough of that you don't have time. Here are your necklaces, they will hold your gratitude tokens till you swap them for energy or something else.' She says while giving us each a mesh silver chain.
- 'Thank you miss.' We all say.
- 'Now off you go and don't be late. Oh, and I'll be taking you back to your place soon, you have work there too don't forget.'
- 'Yes miss, thank you.' We each say goodbye and then go out and join Ad.

He guides us out of the academy and into the city. Our first stop is to be the transport place. Apparently, they sell anything that can take you around, including giant snails with harnesses. Ad'emeiy says that if we really have the energy to pay for it, we can even get enchanted wearable wings that allow one to fly by feeding them little bits of energy. We end up each getting a float board because the wings cost twenty million a pair. I wonder if Master Oska has a pair.

Zipping around on our boards, we go next to the request board and find ourselves a four-person quest. It's quite a basic one, we need to find someone's lost pet, an anteater. For most people that would have been a pain, anteaters are really good at hiding themselves in strange places and staying hidden. The thing is, I can talk to animals with my mind so it's that much easier. I ask E'ls to help me out and we mentally push out our thoughts until we find the creature we are supposed to. On the way, if you can call it that, our mental trip through the city, we stumble across a few quite interesting things and one of them is the protector dragon for the academy. *Have fun out there but be back for curfew youngling.* He says as our minds touch. I say we will be sure to come back in time and just then he points my mind to the famous anteater. I make contact and E'ls'trint tell the animal to go home, he does not want to at first but accepts if we take him there. And so the story goes, we took an anteater back home and got just enough gratitude tokens that we will be able to get all we need for school.

Having fun is clearly not a hard task when flying around the city on a sort of hovering skateboard and getting paid for catching a pet anteater. What seriously makes my day is going to the central crystal bank. It is literally a huge building grown out of hundreds of trees and blocks of crystals. We walk in and are greeted by the warm breath of a baby dragon. Without thinking I reach out with my mind and greet the dragon. *Greetings mighty one.* I say, mimicking a book I read not long ago. *Greetings invoker, I smell something interesting on you, who is your familiar?* Comes a very sweet, clearly young and female voice, directly into my mind. I don't have time to answer before E'ls'trint does so and she then has a huge discussion with the dragon. I end up blocking part of my mental link with E'ls when they start talking about boys.

We walk up to the front desk and immediately I remember the rule of showing our marks. I show mine first and then the banker or whatever I'm supposed to call him shows his. And he then greets me very politely. Something like 'We welcome thee to our establishment.' I don't quite know what to say back so Ad'emeiy joins in, he greets the banker and in turn shows his marks. They are a long strip of little droplets; I guess his element is water.

With all the greetings said and done, we get down to business and exchange our tokens for energy. We take off the tokens we each have on our necklaces and in exchange get given a crystal each that we are to hang in their place. The crystal we can use to pay for things, it allows for protected energy transfers between people. They all glow with different colours, in response to our elements I would think. Mine has a sort of dark spot in the centre turning in the middle of it, probably to represent my 'void' element. Eliya's is crackling with electric flashes and E'ls'trint's is glowing with a little flame in the centre of it. Ad'emeiy's is hardly glowing but is a deep turquoise-blue colour.

After each receiving our crystals and getting a certain amount of energy from the bank, we head to the 'Academic Super Shop for Young Mage Students' or ASSFYMS. Not to be said wrong, I mean seriously, just don't. Well, apart from the strange name we end up walking through the entire shop towards the 'adult' section. Here are the famous crystal tablet things the students all have. It's apparently a magical equivalent to your average tactile tablet with a few perks you're not used to. Functions that I've never had on human tech such as automated four-dimensional renderings. As in it prints a moving three-dimensional object. I'm totally going to have a ball with that. I mean, I can render out anything I design on the tablet, that's just amazing. After a few minutes of discussion with Ad'emeiy we choose our crystal slates and get the necessary licenses with them. It's just a sort of interface, in form of a bracelet, to feed the slate energy. After we have that we get a pen made for each of us, it's like a stylus but it creates its own surface to write on and transfers to the crystal tablet. You can even write in mid-air and it works just fine; the pen will even leave a tiny glow trail you can see but others can't. Of course, all these things draw energy to work but it's ridiculously low. The pen making takes only a few minutes as all they need to do is feed a piece of raw material some energy and then the artisan makes the pen from it. Apparently, they are the best ones we can find and they are made to last for life.

After getting all our materials, we go to the telephone shop or at least the local equivalent and buy a communicator each. They are very thin pieces of crystal and metal worked together in a cool way. They draw off the same bracelet as everything else and don't cost particularly much. The sales girl tells us that people tend to change their communicators quite often as they are also a fashion item so it tends to make people want to change it to suit their desires and trends. The only thing with that is that most people never think to just modify the one they have and thus it's easy to find second, third, or even fourth-hand communicators that are in fact only a year or so old.

Needless to say, after a few more minutes we are exchanging 'signatures', their equivalent of phone numbers but that are marked to the person not the device. In other words, you don't change signature when you change device so that helps.

After all our fun in town, we head back to the academy so that we can make it before curfew.

New Recruits

Only a few days later, some time at the beginning of May, Mrs Lightwind appears one morning to take Eliya and myself back to our home towns for my exams and Eliya's internship. We'll be coming back and forth to Antartis a lot more as Eliya needs to do her full internship and I need to finish my inscription for the master's degree. Just because we are magicians in training does not mean we don't need human training too. And apparently, we'll be set up with a two day, four days, ratio so that we can follow both courses. The only thing is that we may have a hard time doing it all in one go. I am going to look at other options such as correspondence classes to avoid having to portal back and forth all the time. I've not yet mastered my void magic at a good enough rate that I can transport myself and I don't have the correct credentials to enter the magic barriers of the city.

Mrs Lightwind tells us that E'ls'trint will have to stay at the Academy but that our communicators work fine in the human world so we will always be in contact with each other. Apparently, my telepathic link to E'ls is not going to be able to go through the Antartis barriers.

When we have packed a few things and are out in the Academy's court yard, E'ls'trint gives Eliya and me a kiss each, as usual on the lips, and stifling her tears she walks back to the dormitory. She'll be taking notes for all three of us for the next week and a half. Then I'll be back in Antartis but Eliya has to stay at her internship for another four months.

Mrs Lightwind appears in front of us and then, by simply touching us, we are in the void. She walks in this void space, one hand holding Eliya, one hand holding me. Before long, we walk through a sort of opening and are back, in front of the university in my city. It's morning and I've only got a few hours to revise in before my first exam.

'I'll come and get you here in ten days Roarn, good luck for your exams and for your internship Eliya.' Says our professor before disappearing.

Eliya has to dash to the bookshop where she is working before she is late and I'm going to try and memorize all these stupid phonemes I need to know off-by-heart.

Things go much faster than I would have thought they would, within a few minutes I've revised all I needed to for my exams so I decide to go and greet my old friends and classmates without omitting Master Oska. As I'm looking around the Languages building, I find Daphne and Loua in deep discussion. Being my usual self, I walk up to them and say hi and from there things happen pretty fast too. They both look at me as if they've seen a ghost and that's when I remember I'm still dressed in full academy attire, and I have my marks fully visible. At that moment, when I feel utterly stupid for not having changed, and even more than for showing my marks, they greet me. Both forearms bared and marks on full show, they give me a slight bow and say, 'Greetings MT Roarn.' I don't know if I'm more shocked that they know my ranking or that they are both magicians now too or that they are speaking effortless E'rtkinian. I guess a mix of all three. It's only after Master Oska appears out of the building that I understand the situation.

- 'Greetings Master Oska, how have you been?' I say, giving her the traditional mark show.
- 'Quite well thank you and yourself MT Roarn, it's been a while, how are Eliya and your little Vixen?' She replies with the same show of marks.
- 'They are both fine, or at least last I saw they were. I see you have new AMOs, how did that happen.
- Glad to hear that. As for the apprentices, I actually have five at the moment. The royals back in Antartis asked me to recruit at least another fifteen humans into the ways of the E'rtkin so I am following order. The girls were wondering where you had disappeared to so I thought to test them for magic and they had it.
- When are they going to come to the academy then?

- They are not, we've founded an academy explicitly for the human students in the French mountains. You and Eliya are the last human students to go straight to the academy in Antartis; now it will only be on selection.
- I see, that's quite cool. Well, I'm sorry I need to go sit my exams, are you two coming?' I ask Loua and Daphne.
- 'Yeah, let's get going, see you later Master.' Replies Daphne.
- 'See you later Master.' Adds Loua.

And just like that we ended up all in a line sitting in the exam room with two other students of Master Oska, also my classmates from the university. Apparently, they are all students of Master Oska and that is pretty cool because she seems to have chosen a large variety of people.

Before the exam starts, I open up my link to E'ls'trint and crank up the power with my energy but, as I was told, it does not go through at all. I guess the wards around the city prevent telepathic communication as well. Damned, I'll have to ask Master Oska or Mrs Lightwind if there is a way around those protections. Well, for now I'm going to have to pass the exams and then move on to the next ones. I've only got four to do but that is annoying enough as it is. I don't like not being able to talk to E'ls.

Dear readers, not to spread my rage on these pages the author and I consorted with each other and decided that we would omit that and skip to the end of the first day of exams. So, after those annoying exams I went down to the bookshop to find Eliya and see if I could help her with anything even if I'm not really supposed to. Her boss has allowed me to help a little bit when their workload is large and thankfully that's the case today. So, I spend some time helping her out before Master Oska summons us to meet up with her new apprentices. We are the equivalent of three years ahead of them but that does not matter for now as we are just going for a coffee apparently.

When we get to the said coffee shop and go in, Master Oska is waiting for us tapping her watch.

- 'I thought I taught you not to be late and yet you get here four minutes late, what happened?
- Sorry Master Oska, Eliya finished work late so we could not make it any earlier.
- I see, that's alright then. Did you manage to get through to E'ls'trint in the end? I don't think you can get around the wards but you may find a way.
- No, not at all and it's quite a bother. I miss her little voice in my mind.
- Well, you'll be back in Antartis soon enough. Come now you lot we've got a coffee to order and some explaining to do.'

Once seated in the coffee shop, doubling as a book shop for that matter, we order ourselves some lovely warm beverages and cake before Master starts her detailed explanation of the recent events. Due to the massive growth of human population and all the bombings like Manchester, Paris and Brussels and other horrible events, the E'rtkin have had to train more and more environmental magicians to go in and help where they could. They can't stay there and do nothing, it's just not like them. Thus, a few weeks ago, the high council of Antartis voted the opening of a new academy in the centre of France, right in the middle of the Massif Central. The new academy is on a no selection basis, all human students are to go there apart from the ones who were recruited before they founded it. The idea is pretty simple, there will be constant portals set up from all the resident cities of the students and they are to go to their academy as much as they can. All the classes are open and cross level, the only separation comes after the first inter-academy competitions.

Also, a new bit of details we were not originally given, there will now be competitions between the various levels of the academy and between the three academies. They are meant to strengthen our bonds and also make us more agile and powerful. The competitions will all be sports related with hoverboard races, magic tag, intercontinental strategy games and more. I have no idea what form it's all going to take but apparently there will be games every four months.

Another unexpected evolution in recent events is the building threat against the E'rtkin. Because of human technologies and social evolution, they are in constant search of new lands to inhabit. There is one great problem with that, their eyes are turned to the three areas the E'rtkin have built safe heavens: Antarctica, the Moon and Mars. There is talk of revealing the existence of the E'rtkin to the humans again but that seems to be a bad idea. Two factions are building up against each other in that debate and that is an unprecedented event in their history. They are a peaceful people so such a huge separation in ideals is something nearly mythical to them.

Aside from all the recent events, we have a lovely evening and are soon on our separate ways home. I try E'ls'trint one last time but my telepathy seems to be hitting a brick wall that I just can't break. I really hope she is alright; I'll have to hope that Ad'emeiy is looking after her. For now, I've got a few last tests to sit and then it's all over and I'll have my year and my degree.

Taking just enough time to actually study for my exams seems like a waste of time so I just sleep until I'm running late for said exams. Right then, with no other options but to cheat a little, I apply a few basic acceleration spells to myself and run to my exam. I should probably have applied a few levels of cloaking too because I made a few cars stare when I outran them on the road. I make it in time and cast an out of breath drying spell to get rid of my sweat. I could cheat for the exams with the access I have to magic but I don't like lying and it's against E'rtkin policy. I could get stripped of all access to magic and see my marks removed for that. I don't really know what to answer on half the questions and clearly that means that I'm still winded. After a few more minutes to get my breath back and calm down, I manage to access all my memory and finish the test. I should have a pretty good grade for this one as well.

When the day of exams is finally over, I only have a few minutes to go and see Eliya before my portal to Antartis is opened. I'll only actually be back at the academy tomorrow some time as I need to go through a full decontamination but at least I'll be there soon enough. Once I've been to the book shop and had the few minutes I could with Eliya, they were really busy today, I dash to the apartment, get my bag and go to the meetup place. Once there, I find Master Oska waiting for me and tapping her watch to tell me I only just made it on time. She opens my portal and I go through. This time I'm alone and when I get to the access area for the city, I'm feeling pretty lonely. Going through the decontamination area is the most boring thing of all, I have to sit, doing nothing, and cast nearly a hundred purification spells. I know why they have me do this but it's still seriously frustrating.

Oh, damned this is not going to end well...

Yes, dear reader that chapter title has a reason and you'll know why very soon don't worry.

After finally finishing the decontamination spells and taking the transport to the city, I feel E'ls'trint reach out to me mentally.

- 'Roarn, invoke me please. I need to see you now.' He voice is all shaky and sad. I've no idea what happened to her in the past few days but something bad must have happened because she sounds seriously pained.
- 'Come!' I invoke her and she falls into my arms and bursts out crying. 'What's wrong E'ls, you put too many blockers up I can't see what happened in your mind?
- I'll take them down but I need a kiss first, please, I really feel horrible. I just hope you'll still love me after you find everything out.' She is still crying and I can feel her barriers drop but before I look into anything I need to reassure her.
- 'E'ls, my little vixen, I will always love you. Do you want to tell me what happened or should I look?

- I'll let you look; I can't really describe all of it but let's go back to the dormitory first.'

We head back towards the academy and then to our building. It's nearly past time to be in the corridors but too bad for that, we need to get to our room.

As we turn into the last corridor, our supposedly safe area, E'ls'trint's reflexes fire up. I don't understand until it's too late. Someone just launched a spell at the two of us and I have no idea what it is supposed to do. I did not hear the wording nor do I see any immediate effects on either of us. Our energy levels are fine and nothing else seems off so whatever the spell was it either failed or we are in for something really big. We get into our room and that's about as much as I remember.

- 'Okay say that to me again, what happened yesterday night?' Asks Mrs Lightwind. E'ls and I woke up this morning in our suite and we were both naked in each other's arms. We got into our uniform and immediately called out to our supervising professor.
- 'We were walking down the corridor to our room and someone cast an unknown spell at us. Next thing we knew we were awake this morning, in bed together and naked. That would have been nearly okay if we could actually recall what happened.' Answers E'ls.

- 'I suppose you have not yet had time to tell Roarn about the events of that night?' Asks Mrs Lightwind her face downcast.
- 'No, we were on our way to the room so that I could tell him.
- I see, would you be comfortable if I told him? It might be safest if you keep that out of your mind for a few more minutes.
- Yes, you can, I'll wait in the room next door.
- Thank you E'ls, I will call you in a minute.'

Here I am with my supervising professor telling me that my familiar, the other part of my conscious nearly got raped and I don't know what else. The day Eliya and I left for the human world, E'ls'trint felt really down and kept on staying isolated even turning down Ad'emeiy's offer to keep her company. That night, on her way to our room she got pulled into another room and magically drugged. It was a spell meant to make her have a one-hour amnesia she would remember only the next day. She knew what was happening but was also semi paralysed and thus could not defend herself. There is no way to identify who attempted to rape her but one thing is for sure the entire class and in fact the entire academy knows something happened. She managed to defend herself only a few seconds before things would have gone sideways. They did not account for her fast metabolism in the spells. She got out and had to walk naked down the corridor crying. She was so enraged she clawed a few people pretty bad on her way to the room and then crashed inside and fell unconscious on the ground. She was out for nearly a full twelve hours before news really broke out and Mrs Lightwind went into the room and found her sprawled across the floor in really bad shape.

Hearing the narrative of those events only serves to make me extremely angry but also very worked up about what could have happened yesterday night. So, I call E'ls in and as she enters, we drop our barriers and I hug her as tight as I can against me.

- 'I'm limited in what I can do for your memory without authorization from the parliament but it should be enough.' Says the professor.
- 'Whatever works, we need to know what really happened yesterday night and we also need to know who actually did it.' I reply. It's not like I feel ready for whatever I'm going to find out and neither is E'ls but we can't do much about that.
- 'Well, in that case let's go someplace safer than here.'

Mrs Lightwind takes our hands and teleports us to what must be her house. It's a beautiful place but there is no time for sightseeing. She has us undress entirely and lie exactly like we woke up before she starts casting. The length and complexity of the spell tell me it's at least a top-tier spell.

She has changed language at least four times and never stays regular on the rhythm which means she is pushing a lot of energy into the spell. The moment she enounces the last word I feel a huge mental drop and then everything comes flushing back. The torrent of memories is so intense that E'ls and I have to share each other's load. When it stops spinning, we just start crying. There is nothing else we can do; things are a lot worse than anything I could have thought. The spell was only a sound masking one, the rest came when we could no longer hear the casting. The second spell was cast by about five people and had four effects: first to make us forget the entire night, second to make us horny as all hell, third to remove all mental blocks that keep us apart and fourth was one for violence.

The result of these spells is that we went a lot further than we would ever want to. In brief words the spells made us rape each other. It's probably the sickest thing I've ever heard of done to someone but it's especially bad considering the fact that we shared all each other's' feelings at the time which meant that it was actually really good in the moment.

Mrs Lightwind has us tell her in detail everything we can remember and tells us that, no matter what, they will catch the people who did this to us. I don't know if it's because I'm narrating this or simply because I'm dead tired but I can't seem to react how I should. I just cheated on Eliya and what's more I did it with my familiar, yet, with all that taken into account I don't feel as bad as I should.

- 'I don't understand, I should be extremely angry or desperate for revenge or something extreme and yet I don't feel anything that negative. Is there still a latent spell on me?' I ask Mrs Lightwind. She looks perplex and thinks a while before answering.
- 'Did you go through purification upon arriving here? Because if you did then that would explain a lot. The purification spells are meant to correct your anger levels and bring them to null. In other words, you probably are extremely angry but can't feel it because you are under the safeguard of protection and purification spells.' She seems more than sure about what she is saying.
- 'How long will it take to wear off. It's having effect on the two of us so that really does not help. I could always cancel the spells.' I reply. I don't really know if I have the mana to do that sort of thing right now but I suppose it would better than to stay like a feeling deprived zombie.
- 'I recommend you do not remove the spells as that would make you even more vulnerable. Currently the only safe path is for the two of you to stay behind at least three levels of protection spells and to attend class as if nothing happened. I'll let the professors know about this and the parliament too.

- Why the parliament, are they not busy with more important things?
- Because this sort of thing should be impossible in a land devote to pure truth. Now, here are the spells you need to use. They are Master tier protection spells but I am quite sure you can cast them in combined casting.' She hands me a slip of paper with only three lines on it, all using words I only guess to know.
- 'What do these protect us from?' Asks E'ls.
- 'Nearly everything but any attempt to harm you will cost you energy to defend from. If you pass out from the strain, the spells will stop too. So be careful and keep a watch on your marks. If things really start going badly then I suggest you beat it and get back to your dormitory room.'

The period bell goes, E'ls and I hurry up and cast the three protective spell before Mrs Lightwind teleports us to class. We are greeted by a few classmates and quite a few seem surprised to see me. Some even ask me how my human exams went before the teacher comes in. To my utmost astonishment the person walking in is not our teacher at all by Master Oska and she has Eliya with her. She greats the class and then sends Eliya to join E'ls and me at the front-row seats.

Other than their appearance I nearly fall off my chair when she starts telling the entire class that there are criminals among them and that the parliament has sanctioned an entire decade of exile to the culprits. She then looks at us with a very curious face and says something I don't catch. I hear someone at the back of the class yelp in pain and then a huge holographic projection comes up in the middle of the room. The projection is something I really did not want to see or hear or ever experience. Someone filmed while E'ls'trint was being desecrated. Her frail shape being denuded at the rate of a hand's rapid stokes. Before the hologram can continue E'ls casts a force stop on it and destroys the viewing crystal. She leans onto Eliya's shoulder and cries and that's when the uproar starts.

At the back of the classroom, the person who had the video gets bound to his chair and so do nearly twelve other students. Some people are coming to see E'ls to offer words of kindness and some even offer to cast protection spells on her. And others come up to me and want to yell at me for not protecting my familiar properly, it's my job to protect her and the fact that I did not prove I'm a useless master. E'ls reminds them that I can't act through the protection barriers of the city.

When Master Oska comes up to me, piercing through the barrier of my classmates, she simply says that all copies of the hologram have been recuperated and destroyed and they have pinpointed whose room it was. I am now, in virtue of the ancient laws, allowed to be first to interrogate him on his actions. The parliament is trying their best to figure out how this sort of action could have happened and, in the meantime, they want us not to act on our grudges but to stay put until they can sort out the situation properly.

Contrary to what I originally expected, the room where the events took place is that of a girl. She is there and so is the perpetrator of the aggression on E'ls'trint and possibly on me too. I go in alone and he immediately starts casting spells at me. The barriers hold and his spells disintegrate.

- 'Unless if you can keep that up all day, I suggest you stop now before I have to make you look like an idiot.' I say as the fifth ball of fire disintegrates against my shielding.
- 'What the hell are you protected with? Nothing your level should be able to stop my modified armour piercing flames. It's not like I'm going to own up to anything if that's what you were hoping for. I know you were told the E'rtkin can't lie but that's not actually true, we can as long as we are often in the human world.' The purification spells are still too strong, I know I should feel like murdering this bastard and yet I don't. Maybe I really should cancel them.
- 'Trust me you will talk and you will tell me everything I need to get you exiled or better to get your marks striped. You'll have a hard time coming into Antartis if you don't have your marks to grant your access.
- You don't have the authority to do that, only the royals can order a mark removed and it has not been done for

nearly two millennia. Oh, and by the way, I'll make your life hell if you do anything to me.

- There's very little you can do if you can't use your magic. And if I need a royal court order to strip your marks then I'll get one but you are not getting away with this. Now, enough crap and get talking.'

I don't get time to say anything more, Mrs Lightwind appears in the room with a greying man and women. They both bear their forearms to me and I reply in kind. On both of their left arms, they have a tiny crown at the centre of their marks. I guess this is the royal authorization I needed to get rid of his marks. There is not a word exchanged, they look at the boy sitting on his bed tied down by magic, free him and then clamp their hands around his head. Within a few seconds, he is sweating and soon after that he is crying. Serves him right. Damned those purification spells are really messing with my head. His marks are disappearing slowly, retracting into his skin. I can see that it's not causing him any physical pain but the mental strain seems pretty horrible.

After a few more minutes, the two royals let go of him and simultaneously declare: 'Because of your violation of our laws, culture and ways, your aggression on E'ls'trint and Roarn, you are hereby banished from the E'rtkin world. You may never return to any of our cities and will be executed on sight if you try anything else. All your magic has been reduced to only basic level and you will never get anything more. Goodbye.' They say no more before Mrs Lightwind teleports them away. Master Oska then comes in, opens a portal and pushes the guy through. I did not even get his name but that is of no importance now. He is someplace in the human word, lost and totally defenceless, I suppose that will be enough.

Walking out of the room, I hear the girl whose room it is yelling and swearing and I don't know what. I guess she is also partly implicated in the situation as it is her room. E'ls'trint and Eliya are in the corridor waiting for me and as soon as I am there, they both jump at me and hug me. I don't quite understand why but I'm happy that Eliya is not trying to kill me first. I guess I could not do anything about what happened so we need to get over it now. I'm going to have to pay attention as much as possible in class to keep my mind off this whole story. One thing is certain, the mental bond between E'ls'trint and I is now excessively strong. I feel everything she does and know all she knows. It's going to be complicated getting used to being two people.

Back to a Normal Life

Eliya went back a few days after those incidents and has only been here a few days over the past three months. Soon though, she shall be here for a bit longer. I've been writing to her nearly every day with my modified tablet. It talks to human satellites while remaining invisible to them. Sure, we have our communicators but that is not very discreet out in the human world, at work. The incident has passed into silence but for some reason I know it's going to swing back at us soon.

Over the past three months E'ls and I have been taking cram classes and extracurricular classes until we needed extra hours in the day. It's got to the point where I let her go to hers with her boyfriend and I go to mine while we share all the learnt knowledge. Yes boyfriend, she is dating Ad'emeiy and has been for a few weeks already. He is really a good bloke and has been looking after her and given her what she needed, love and lots of it. Other than the extra classes to hone our skills and gain as much knowledge as we can, I've made a few really good friends in the class whom I get to spend time with. Things are really going well and I've even managed to fit in quest time. Often, I go with friends or with E'ls and Ad, those two are really good for many quests and we are now going to get accreditation for the higher-level ones. I still need to sit the theoretical exams to be a top-tier mage but that will come soon too. E'ls is passing the high tier tests and Eliya is on the same ones as me. I've been transmitting all the classes to her as best as I can. With all my time spent on learning things and going on missions, I really did not see my life change, my body change and my entire world change actually. Things have been going ever so fast and with such little time wasted on details that I nearly missed the biggest changes. Out of all the things that could have gone wrong in my life, many of them ended up going right and I'm now living a normal student life.

E'ls and Ad'emeiy have been preparing their exams and the next part in their life, that of union. I had no idea until E'ls let me see the memory of Ad asking her to be his wife. Things like that don't happen often and when they do it calls for major celebration. Eliya is arriving the day after tomorrow so I've got until then to ready a few things for her, make a nest for E'ls and get the rest of the necessities out. I've convinced the board to let Eliya and I change room so that we are next to Ad'emeiy and E'ls'trint's. In a normal human life that would mean moving all our stuff down the corridor and all those lovely things; in an E'rtkin life, it just means casting the transportation spells on the doors and letting the magic do the rest. My void magic is really one of the most useful things I could have got, it allows for a lot of energy efficient transportation magic. I've been practising some invocation magic with E'ls and I'm also looking for loopholes in my protection spells that would allow me to make them more powerful for less mana hungry.

Next week, when Eliya is here we are going to try and complete our next level exams and thus be top tier mages, that would allow us to enter the class with our age group in it without being a level or two lower than them. I'm thinking of all the ways this could go wrong, a new habit I have since the less savoury events of the past. It's strange, though, when talking about my school life, I need to remember that I'm going to be doing a Master's degree in the human world but a master-level course in the E'rtkin world. Those being two substantially different things. I've also lost the right to use the speed learning spells that we were taught when we started learning the E'rtkinian ways; according to Master Boulan the excessive use of speed learning and hyper memorization magic can do long-term damage that even the legendary healers can't fix.

After all my classes are done, I go to the eating hall and reserve my usual space at the end of one of the tables and wait for E'ls and Ad'emeiy to arrive. Before they get here, someone I've never met before appears and sits down next to me, Eliya's usual spot.

- 'Hi Roarn, we've been watching you for a while and would like to know if you want to join our table.' Says the stranger. He did not show his marks so I don't either, even if I feel that I should. I do not have the faintest idea of whom he speaks for but something tells me I should be weary of what could motivate his act of kindness.
- 'Hello, may I know whom you speak for? And also, what is your name?' I'm actually kind of surprised that he has not given me that information before extending his offer.
- 'Oh yeah, I forgot about those bits. I am Irrwen of Avalon one of the knights of the mythical cities. It's a long pompous name to say we are all striving to reach the forgotten cities. To enter our group, you need to have legendary potential and actually try to make it that far. The potential is obviously not enough.
- So, wait, you are actually a real descendant of Avalon or is that just part of the name?
- Nope, that's my surname. You have been progressing at such a rate that we can only hope you will continue and fulfil your potential. Would you join our table and discuss all of these things with us?
- Can my familiar and her boyfriend come as well?
- Of course, the invitation extends to them and to your soulmate as well.'

I nod and follow him to the table on the far end of the room where a bunch of people, boys and girls alike are laughing and throwing minor spells at each other. One of the girls has a huge sword next to her encrusted with gleaming crystals. Irrwen sits down next to her and people shuffle to the sides to make space for me at the table across from Irrwen and the girl with the sword. She bares her marks and says her name is A'lyse. I reply in kind and soon I'm in deep discussion about the purpose of their group and how they do what they do.

Soon after we start discussing the existence of a flying city that goes by the name of Liberia, E'ls'trint and Ad'emeiy arrive at the table and greet everyone. To my utter surprise E'ls'trint seems to have quite some affection for A'lyse, so much so that I can't not look at her. That's the problem with being mentally linked to my familiar is that I not only sense what she senses but I feel all she feels too. The problem is I can feel her boyfriend is less amused by my stare, he does not know there is little I can do about it, as long as E'ls feels attracted I will too. Even though our meal is of the usual excellency I almost don't taste it as we are all deep in conversation.

When our meal is over, I go with A'lyse and Irrwen as well as a few others from their group to the big library where we hunt down the books on Liberia and borrow a few each. On the way back to the dormitory, E'ls comes up to me and asks if she can sleep in my bed as she wants to talk to me. Obviously, that means no one must know about it, since the less savoury event we have been sure not to spend too much time alone together. It pains us both enormously to remain separate like this but there is very little we can do for that. Things are complicated enough we don't need anyone reminded of what happened nor do we wish to have it brought to mind too often.

Once back at the dormitory I first make the move that I needed to, transferring one room to the other and thus Ad'emeiy's room and my room are next to each other. Some things I need to move by hand but that will not take especially long so I get cracking. Thankfully, the only things I need to move by hand are the magically locked boxes we use to safeguard our energy crystals and other powerful items. To move those, I need to first remove a few dozen levels of protection spells and thus it takes some time.

Interesting Events

That night, after everyone had gone to sleep and the hallways are on lockdown, I call for E'ls and invoke her into my room. Unsurprisingly she is not wearing anything and she immediately jumps into my bed and snuggles herself in. No matter what she tries and how much effort she puts in, she will always be an adorable little vixen. I get my things ready for tomorrow and then get to bed.

- 'So, what's up? It's been a while that you have not wanted to spend a lot of time with me.' It's strange how much we miss each other even if we share half of our feelings. I don't know how the familiar system is supposed to work but one thing is for sure, it's not meant for separation.
- 'I've been distant for only one reason; I can't keep things from you if we are together all the time.
- It's not like you need to keep things from me. What is it that you want to tell me?
- Well, according to the academy healer, I am pregnant.' Oh, I did not see that coming. How on earth am I supposed to react in a situation like this I wonder?

- 'I have no idea how to react. I'm really happy for you and at the same time worried about how you will manage the situation. I mean being a mommy is going to be complicated.
- I know that and I also knew you would not be sure how to react so don't worry just be the master I know you as. You can say what you like I will accept anything. Also, I shall be taking a small break in my schooling to bring up my child but that will not be a problem as I follow all the classes through your eyes.
- Are you sure that this is a situation you wish to be in at such a young age, though?
- I am not young; in fox standards I should already be on my fourth or fifth carriage. And yes, I am sure.
- Well, then all I can do is support you and your child to my utmost best. I'm just wondering, how long is your gestation going to be?
- The healer has no idea and, this bit I did not want to share, they are not sure who the father is. Apparently, it's possible that it is you.' That would be something of a horrible situation. Not only did things become strange between her and I because of what happened but if she is carrying my child, it would be impossible to fix.
- 'How can they not know who the father is, I mean it has to be Ad'emeiy right? It's not like you two have not been active in that domain.' The inconvenient part about

sharing all feelings is that I also know when she is making love with her boyfriend.

- 'Yes, it should be but because they can't tell how long my gestation will be, they can also not know who the father is. Worst of it all, apparently none of their detection spells can understand my strange physiognomy and thus they are at a loss for any more information.

- I see, and when will you get that information? Without being funny it will be very hard for both of us if we have a child together. I don't think our partners will appreciate is somehow.' I am in fact quite certain that it would bring absolute chaos into our lives.

E'ls does not pursue that subject any longer and rather changes it telling me that we can only wait and see. We talk about our recent quests and the few we are waiting for. There will soon be an inter-academic tournament and we need to have a load of quest points to apply for it. The two of us have nearly enough but, because Eliya was not here for a while, she will need a load more points and we can share ours with her so quests here we come.

That night, contrary to what I would have thought with the prior announcement, I sleep like a log with my little fox tucked up against me. And the next morning, I teleport her back to her room. I've only recently been able to properly send her to other places than ones I can see but it seems that, by combining both of our powers, we can get her to nearly any location of her choice and that is really a useful bit of work.

We go to the dining hall together that morning and Eliya surprises us by being at the table with A'lyse and Irrwen. She nonchalantly motions us over and gives me an epic kiss when I get there. E'ls gives her a huge hug too and then says 'hi' to the rest of the table. Once all the greetings are done, we settle into breakfast and bring Eliya up to speed about the latest details. I'm so happy to see Eliya that poor E'ls'trint's tail is waiving all over the place. Truly, I am happy that I do not have an emotionally triggered appendix like that, it would drive me crazy. Once everyone has shared their finds about Liberia, we discuss the upcoming tournament and many people at the table start discussing alliances and unit formations. I don't understand all of it but for the part that I do understand they are all looking forward to the events and are more than qualified to participate. A'lyse has nearly a thousand times more quest points than what is needed to enter. 'My parents used to give me chores in quest format so that I could win points faster.' She explains.

We are soon heading to our classes and thus some file out as they are not in the same age group as us. This is the second last week of class before a month-long break in which the tournament will take place. Once settled into class, in our front row seats, Eliya, E'ls, Ad'emeiy and myself start discussing the more trivial parts of our life at the academy and the developments of our powers. I've done a few studies on my strange power at changing human technologies into E'rtkin ones and have made a lot of progress in void magic but pure energy is nearly impossible to study and alteration is somehow hard to come by. That makes two of my magics that I can't really study and one that no one understands. Eliya has been learning a lot about her three elements, electricity, rock and light, she has even brought two of them to near-master level. As for E'ls'trint, well hers is a little more complex, some of the spells she is trying to learn do not just work, they need to be altered to her physiognomy. Though that does not matter too much, her fire magic is now at top tier level and her plant magic is not far behind. She can make an entire tree grow from seed simply by feeding it her energy. In retrospect we are now full-fledged members of the E'rtkinian society and have magic powers high enough to be seen a superior by some.

When our professor walks in, I'm not surprised to see a large floating bulletin board come in behind him. What is more surprising is that the tournament is starting in three hours not three days. The board is showing the teams and apparently, we will not be choosing our teams nor will there be any changes made. Each Antartis student is set with a student from each of the other two academies. In other words, we, friends, will be in competition against each other. Thus implying that, no matter what, we can't form any alliances at will, there are going to be complications.

'The first part of the tournament is a treasure hunt race across the entire planet. You will be wearing bracelets with your team number on them and they render you invisible to the human eye. You are allowed to use any magic you choose to battle and search for the two hundred treasures but you must include a non-destructive and non-harming part to each of them. Also, you will not know who is on your team unless you check their bracelet. Lastly, if you lose a team member then you will have one randomly assigned from a team in the same situation.' Those are the first explanations we are given. Seconds after, a bracelet appears in front of each of us and we clamp them on to our wrists. We exchange numbers with Eliya, E'ls, Ad, A'lyse and Irrwen before it's too late. This way we can help each other find our groups.

'There will be no details given as to the location of the treasures, only that they are all across the globe. They each have an energy beacon on them that will last for two weeks, after that the beacon dissipates and the treasure is teleported back here. You are forbidden access to the academy for the duration of the first trial and thus classes are postponed to after the games. Lastly, you need to know the following: you will be classified on your abilities during the trials and each one will bring a number of points to your team. Students from the other academies can win a place here in Antartis if they get enough points just like you can lose your place if you get too little.' That creates a huge uproar to the point where the professor casts a silence spell on the room. 'Each one of the treasures has the rules for the second trial with it, thus if you fail the first trial you fail the second as well. Unless if you manage to capture another team's treasure.' Before that goes any further, the professor opens a portal and leaves the room. I keep on forgetting that portal magic is a speciality but also a base magic. In other words, we are going to have to use it a lot to find our group and our treasures.

When no one seems to move E'ls gives our group each a kiss and then, pulling on my void magic, disappears from the room. I offer to take the group with and we go directly to the new academy in France. Thankfully, my recent studies have allowed me to bypass wards using my void magic for transportation. I can now also take people with me. We don't have time to go past our rooms and pick things up, the games are already starting.

The Trials

There are many complications when one is looking for but two people on a planet with over seven billion. We have been sharing our various ideas on how to track down the members our teams and for the moment no one has come up with anything that actually works. We decided to form a temporary alliance while we look for the rest of our various teams. At least the location of the academy in France is not very hard to find, they have an energy signature that is visible from halfway across the country. When we get there E'ls'trint is walking towards the gates, from the inside, with five other people. *I found all of your group members, they got given the location of the other academy so we are headed there next.* She tells me telepathically. We greet our team members and then, with a bit of energy from each of them, I open a void portal and we hop in. We walk through the void space for only a few seconds before coming out by a cave entrance. I guess this is the entrance to the academy no one has really heard much about. It's nearly a myth back in Antartis and I've only heard a few scary things about it. Apparently, all the extremely high danger magic is taught here. That does mean that there should not be any permanent students here. In reality we have no idea what on earth we are to expect in anything given to us by the professors. I mean, if they are anything as sadistic as what the other students say, this could be one gigantic trap.

Little choice do we have so here we are, our ten-man group, walking into the unknown-cave-of-doom-academy. It does not even have a name and I think that is probably the scariest part of it all. Not only is there no documentation on this place but it does not even have a name.

Upon walking in, magic lights come on all around us and a huge group of students is there, waiting for us. They are all about our age but look totally different to anything I've ever seen. I'm quite sure I should say that they are aliens but that would be incorrect, they are E'rtkin but I think they are just quite a lot further from the world than we thought. Their expressions are full of knowledge and judgement but also passion, caring and I think plain common love in a few cases. The next few seconds are crazy: there is a frenzy of hugs, gifts and a lot of magic energy moving all around us. They greet us each in a very strange way, they show us their marks like we do but they then bring them to life with energy. It's as if their marks were alive.

'Welcome to the E'rtkin underworld, we are all selected students for the inter-magic games and will be guiding you for the treasures found in our world. Call out your team number and we will join you.' Says one of the older looking students.

The fact that he is mentioning underworld is not something I have any understanding of so I'll just tell you this, I don't trust them. It seems fundamentally wrong that there should be an underworld for the E'rtkin but then again, I don't exactly know all of their history.

We start calling out our numbers and finding the last members of our groups and right after we are off. I get a last kiss from Eliya and a lick from my vixen before we all dash into portals and off to the rest of the world.

My team and I walk through the void, yes, I still need to explain how that is possible. Basically, the void is a non-dimensional space, in other words, there is neither time nor position there. When I enter it or pass something through it, my mana creates those dimensions for the duration of travel. Also, I can place things in the void and pull them out again later using the same sort of principle, it's useful but complicated. Needless to say, we walk through the void and stop in northern Canada. We decided we would search each continent as we go.

The biting cold hits us immediately and nearly knocks us off our feet. A blizzard is blowing past and we are going to have to spend far too much mana to try and protect ourselves. 'Cast a void shield Roarn.' Says Lumina the girl from the E'rtkin underworld School. I've no idea what she means but I still understand the idea and try a few wordings before casting my magic out. I did not give it a direction but rather a shape, I made a millimetre thick veil around us linked directly to the void. I have no idea how we are going to cast any spells through a void barrier but we shall see I suppose. A few seconds later I hear Lumina and Alexander dual casting a shield spell and as soon as it's up I take mine off. Their shield only prevents the cold wind from hitting us and the snow flies around us instead of onto us. With those spells in place and running on low mana, we actually start talking to each other starting with a bit more of the basics.

- 'So, we've only exchanged first names, and other than that we don't know each other. If we are to simultaneously cast spells and reinforce each other then I guess we'd better get ourselves into a more coherent form.' Says Lumina with a bit of a smile.
- 'Well, then who wants to go first?' I ask.
- 'I'll go. My name is Lumina Lightwood, my main magic element is light and I have a small ability at time modification as well.
- I'm Alexander Gale and I have a strong affinity with the element of earth.
- And I'm Roarn Rogue, I'm a void manipulator and animal telepath mainly. It's a pity she is in an opposing team but I have a familiar that turned herself into a human, you guys would have liked her I'm sure of it.

- That sounds like a load of fun.' Says Lumina. 'What shall we do next? Get the rest of these markers we are supposed to find?
- Well, that would be a good idea yeah, I must say. Can you guys keep up the shielding? If you can, I can warp us to all locations we sense these things at.
- Yeah, I can keep 'em up fine, they only draw when we are in danger and they draw on environmental energy in any way.' Says Alexander.
- 'Same for me; but, will they be able to pass through the void without disappearing?
- Yep, not a problem, don't worry, I bubble us when we go through. I can void walk without protection but you guys would probably disintegrate.
- That would not be fun so let's avoid that, shall we? Replies a slightly unhappy Alexander.
- Yeah, I'm not up for it either. Says Lumina.'

On those words, we are off. We literally bounce all over the planet and in the underworld too finding these beacon things by the dozen pretty fast. Seems like the other teams are doing really well too because there are quite rapidly none left to find. Once we have not found any in three hours, we warp back to the large "neutral zone" and find most of the other teams there. I open the telepathic barriers and find E'ls'trint and her team pretty fast, we walk to them and she gives me a huge hug and then greats all the rest of my team as I greet hers. Seems she has four more beacons than us.

It takes some time before Eliya and her team make it back; though when they do it's a crazy arrival. They breach space in the middle of us all and drop down with a bag full of beacons. Clearly, they won but this is more than a win, it's madness. She comes up to me and I smell the burn and the ice and more on her, they found some of these in lava, in an avalanche and in a lot of other crazed places. Their beacons are probably the hardest ones to find.

"Did you guys have to put one on the ISS? I scared the crap out of the dudes up there when I dropped out of thin air into the space station." She says to the headmasters and organizers. They just laugh at that and seem to be more impressed than anything else.

The results speak for themselves, Eliya and her team are first with four hundred points and a bit, next is E'ls and her team with two hundred and fifty and my team is fourth after a team I don't even recognize, we have a hundred and twenty points. Once that is sorted, we are told to go wherever we like and rest for twenty-four hours. The five top teams join up and we warp off to a little tropical island off the coast of Madagascar called Reunion. There, we find a hotel near the beach and check into an entire floor. Helps when you can create an endless amount of cash that is not even fake.

Hope or a new way of being?

As we are partying in our victory and happy about it, temporary couples seem to form between the people that are single. I have a bad feeling about the fact that Ad'emeiy is not here so I let E'ls pull on my void magic and go and get him and his team. They check in a few minutes later and we now have a full floor of crazy E'rtkinian kids playing around with elemental magic in a human hotel. We blanked all the tech so that we are invisible and have been mucking about ever since. I've brought some things with from home and thus we are really being crazy. At some point, we receive a message telling us to be ready in twelve hours for the next part of the games so we crash for the night, at three in the morning.

Waking up in a king-size bed with my Eliya is a great way to start a day, what makes it a little less cool is to see that we are running late. After a ten second magic shower and change we gather in the lobby, give in our key cards and warp out. I am transporting all of us so it's a bit of a strain but that's a small price to pay for us to get to the meeting point on time.

We make it and are welcomed with the crowd of other students and organizers.

'The next challenge is the hardest of the three, says the headmaster, you are to all join forces and build a new country for the E'rtkin people. You have twelve days to manage this feat though it must be done off earth soil so up to you guys to decide how you will do it.' It's said with such calm statement that he can only be serious even if it sounds crazy. The organizers leave after that with, in their stead, a huge crystal table that we can plan on and a codex of transformation spells. Many people seem taken aback but then comes a single line message to all of us: 'We are at war with the humans we need to leave.' That's a pretty bland way to say that our world is going to crumble and they need an escape route. We are to create an entire city, off world and preferably entirely independent from Earth. Word spreads and soon there is a part of the group that breaks off in chaos but not all of it thankfully.

Planning starts soon after that and we take a vote for location: Mars wins by a huge margin. It's going to be tough to get all of us there and more specifically not to die in the process so we start by organizing a supply route and a load of harvesting groups set out to get as many earth specimens as possible. I'm part of the so called 'pioneer group' because I'm one of two void users and we are the only one to be able to make it to the red planet without dying halfway there. With some help, we take a total of eight people into the void and with us a bubble of air to last five days. In that time, we need to create our first habitat on our new world using mainly alchemic magic and our own energy. It takes a few hours of void walking to make it there but when we do it becomes clear that our trip will be one of many. Casting a dozen layers of shielding, we step onto Mars soil.

'Well, that was underwhelming, says E'ls, I was expecting some sort of huge storm or something but nope, nothing but silence.' I smile and pull out the oldest sentence in the book: 'One small step for us and a leap for the rest of 'em.' Not exactly like the original but it's better to invent my own stuff, is it not?

We start our years of work with an impossible amount of hope. Hope that we will be right about our choice. Hope that we will reach that ideal of peace we strive for. Hope that we will save the E'rtkin people who have put their hope in us. More than anything, hope that this is not all in vain. Oh, and let's not forget, hope that we can survive this challenge in 12 days and then make it for the last challenge. The fact that it took nearly 200 years to make the sanctuaries and we have 12 days tells me that they are expecting a lot from us.

First comes the creation of glass from sand and light and electricity. There are hundreds of spells that we could use but brute force overrules them all and thus we shape brute energy into the glass dome we need and make do with that. It ends up being massive and encompasses approximately ten hectares if I'm not mistaken. We made it be an actual bubble so that the earth's porosity would not be a problem. Next, we have to make something that will convert the air into breathable air and that is a tough amount of work. As we all sit down and start writing the runes on the ground, a communication comes in.

- 'This is Mars sanctuary, you have just appeared outside of the sanctum, are you alive?' Comes a slightly static voice.
- 'Greetings Mars sanctuary, we are alive and well thank you. We are preparing an expansion of the E'rtkin habitat here on Mars would you like to join us in the effort?' Eliya asks back.
- 'Why certainly little Eliya, I hope you're all doing well, nice glass bubble by the way. I'll be there now.' I have no idea who that is until she appears in front of us. It's Mrs Lightwind.
- 'Hello teacher, came to see that we did not die yet?' I ask without being entirely ironic. She smiles, nods and then drops a book in front of us.
- 'This is the full codex for air alchemy, if you lot manage to make it a robust system that can produce constant atmosphere, we will bring everyone else up to Mars and have them make it big enough to convert all Mars air

into breathable air.' As often she does not tally on words and disappears pretty fast thereafter. Of course, offering to help would defeat the purpose of the second challenge.

We get cracking on the codex and interestingly it does not seem complete to any of us so we add in our bits, modify the fragile bits and in the end cast our spell. The ground gives us very little actual diversity in material but we use what we have and transform it into what we need and soon there is a strange tubular machine in the middle of our improvised workstation. One of our group members directs light onto it and it gives off a small hum as it starts to suck in air a lot faster than we thought it would. Placing it in the centre of the bubble, we back up and watch it work for a few minutes before getting to building another four of them that we place all around the bubble. The carbon they pull out the air is pushed into a little reservoir on the side for later use.

- 'Should we get some more people here or should we first build a few things?' Asks E'ls. She is quite obviously missing her boyfriend and for that I understand her and open a void portal.
- 'Go get those whom you think we could use and anything that could make our life here a bit easier like energy crystals from the bank.' I reply.

- 'And please bring us back some coffee.' Says Eliya. The rest of our group nodding along. Doesn't mater what society you are in, coffee is fuel!

The other void user joins E'ls and they go on their way back to Earth.

As we wait for them to come back, a few good ideas take place and more specifically are put in place. We make a few small glass bubbles linked together where we make an air hydrogenator; horrible name to say it's a thing that turns air into water by adding converted hydrogen it gets from the ground. With water we can do a lot more and thus we have to replicate all the machines we make quite a few times subsequently draining our strength. 'Master, we're nearly back, we have food and drink and a load of harvested goods.' Says E'ls over our link; no idea how it is working from within the void but we'll figure that out later. A few minutes after that a void portal appears off the side of the bubble and out of it come a dozen E'rtkin. They have two huge energy crystals with them and what looks to be an entire tropical rain forest of trees and plants.

Over the next few hours we dig, plant and water all the harvested trees while the specialists transform them to adapt to Mars soil. It's not the most time-effective technique and seems not to be efficient in general so we need to figure out some other solution. Someone comes up with a transformation spell that could convert Mars soil into more plant-friendly soil so that is what we use. Drawing on the crystals the spell takes hold pretty fast and drains both crystals but we then have earth-like soil and the plants can thrive in it. Having drained that much energy, we gather together on the fresh grown grass, have a makeshift dinner and then go to crash for the night. E'ls, Ad'emeiy, Eliya and I go off in our direction and make ourselves a nest to sleep in.

The next day comes and we continue using all our combined knowledge, power and strength to make our people a new haven of peace.

It takes us the full twelve days we were given to make a place that is both big enough and safe enough for our people to move into. They are going to fly here in a huge ship that was built in the underground of Antartis and that will be most of the population and as much energy and products they can bring. We have no idea how well their flight will go nor do we know how long it's going to take, what we know is that our world, the E'rtkin world, will not end today.

The END.